DEADWOOD
DAYS

DEADWOOD DAYS

Steven Merrill Ulmen

"Steven Ulmen is a new western writer with promise. In *Deadwood Days,* he proves he is on the right track." – Elmer Kelton

To my Ida Mae, two Matthews, Angela, Amanda, Laura, Pauly, and now, Sophia Pearl and Charlotte Opal

CHAPTER ONE

High overhead, a shaft of sunlight pushed through the clouds, bringing with it a warm light to the men. With the warmth and light came the scream of an eagle as it lit from its nest and glided upwards on the rising currents of air. David Stewart gazed at Ryker, lying in peaceful repose. His face still carried a smile, which was unusual, for in death, an ordinary man's muscles relaxed, expressionless. But then, David knew that nothing about Toby Ryker had been ordinary. Glancing skyward, the eagle reminded him of the old man's previous words: *Oh, look at the king of the skies, David. Sailing and soaring above his domain. Like a free spirit rising, he is. When it's all over for me, here, I hope that is the feeling I'll have!* David sensed that Ryker's spirit was now one with that eagle, freed from the bonds of earthly concerns, and took comfort in knowing this was the way the mountain man wanted it to end. He sighed, replaced his hat, and squinted at the bird until it disappeared from view.

"He was a fine man," David said to the sheriff. "Larger than life in so many ways. The best I ever knew. He taught me how to survive out here." Raising his bandanna, he wiped the tears from his eyes. "He even taught me I could do this without feeling like less of a man."

The sheriff shifted uncomfortably. "The best," he murmured. "Are you going to take him back to your ranch for burial?"

David glanced around the countryside. "No Jesse, I'm not. Toby loved these mountains. He felt at home up here. This is where he fell so this is where he'll stay. I'll bury him under a rock cairn that I'll build right here, and then I'll bring up a tombstone later."

"What will you put on his tombstone?" Jesse asked, pulling out a sack of tobacco and rolling a smoke.

David thought about that one a while before he answered. "Well, I'm not certain of his year of birth so I'll just put 1885 as his date of death. As for an epitaph, I'll have it read 'Western Pioneer.'"

"Toby Ryker, Western Pioneer." Jesse nodded. "Fittin'. That says it all, David."

"Gee, thanks, fellers."

David and Jesse looked at each other. "You say that?" David asked.

"Nope." Jesse raised his eyebrows. "You?"

"Sure didn't, and McQuiston's talking days are over." David glanced down at the old man. "Toby?"

Ryker opened his eyes and pushed the blanket from under his chin. He smiled up at the two men as he studied their shocked faces.

"Toby!" David dropped to his side. "We thought you were dead!"

"No, but this here flesh wound does tingle a bit," Ryker said.

"Flesh wound!" It was Jesse's turn to come unglued. "You got a hole in your chest! There's blood all over you!"

"Well now, not really," Ryker said. "See, when I tried to shoot McQuiston the second time," he motioned to the body of the dead bounty hunter lying fifteen feet away, "his bullet creased me just before I pulled the trigger. It knocked me down and busted this here bottle of ketchup I was totin' around inside my coat. That's the red you're seein'. The slug ripped my coat and scraped off some of my flab, but all things considered, reckon I'm feeling pretty good."

"Ryker, what are you up to? Why did you play dead?" David said.

The old man gulped. He knew David only referred to people by their last names when he was hopping mad. "Well, you see, David, I was so impressed with how kind you were to me and all that I wanted to play out the full hand. I wanted to know if what you promised me yesterday was real. When you said you and the family would tend to me in my old age with my heart attacks and all, I wanted to know if it was real or if it was all a bunch of sheep dip."

"Ryker, you toyed with me."

"Aw, come on now, you mean to tell me that you ain't overjoyed that I'm still alive? And my handle is Toby! Go on! Say it! It's easy, T-O-B-Y!"

David looked from Ryker to Jesse in disbelief.

"Leave me out of this," Jesse said. "He's your friend."

David paused a moment, considering the sheriff's words before he smiled at Ryker. "Right you are, Jesse. He is my friend. Come on Toby, let's get you home." When the old man grinned back, it was the biggest, brightest grin that the rancher had ever seen.

Ryker licked his lips. "That sounds like a fine idea, but let's have us some vittles first. The sheriff looks like he's downright starved." He rolled to one side to stand up but fell back onto his bedroll. "Hmm, this may be a problem. Ain't sure I can walk, David."

The men turned their attention to Ryker and examined him in detail, checking for broken bones, cracked ribs, and the like. After removing his shirt and cleaning him up as best they could, they saw that the bullet indeed caused a flesh wound but did not penetrate any vitals. Why he was unable to stand was a mystery to them. Since the breakfast meal awaited them, they ate and after cleaning up, prepared to break camp. Ryker tried again to stand and this time was successful, but had extreme pain in his back and told David that sitting a horse would be nigh onto impossible. "I think firing from a lying position and taking that slug jolted my back," he said.

David used Ryker's bedroll to rig a travois that Wino, Ryker's horse, was most willing to pull. Thus rigged, they slung the corpse of John McQuiston over his horse and tied it down. They then attached the carcass of the elk that David and Ryker had shot this hunting trip to the pack mule. After breaking camp, they headed down the Medicine Bow Mountains to David's Wells Fargo swing station, located between Woods Landing and Laramie.

Because of Ryker's condition, it was slow going for the men. The travois allowed for relatively comfortable transportation for the huge old mountain man, but the rig was designed for the plains and not for narrow mountain trails. It was necessary for Sheriff O'Brian to lead Wino and for David to bring up the rear, frequently elevating the travois poles into a stretcher around sharp bends and twists in the trail. It took two days to get to the plain below. By late morning on the third day, they entered the yard of the Stewart ranch.

Ida Mae Stewart, David's wife, and their children, Matthew, now 14, Laura, and Pauly, now 9 and 5 respectively, saw them coming a long ways off and were waiting for them when they arrived. Ida Mae ran up to David and hugged him, trembling. "I was so worried," she whispered.

"I'm fine, but we have a complicated situation here, Ida Mae," David said.

"I can see that," Ida Mae replied, pulling the children back from staring at the corpse of the bounty hunter. The body was covered with flies and was ripe and starting to bloat. "Quit gawking at that body," she admonished them. "He's dead. He can't hurt you. But his remains deserve at least some respect."

"First things first," the sheriff said. "Let's get Ryker into the house."

David moved over to the travois. "Toby?"

Ryker opened his eyes. "Huh? Oh, hello David." He glanced around at the others and smiled. "Guess I must have dozed off."

"We got plenty of help here now to get you into the house," David said.

"Well okay. I'm still awful stiff but my back doesn't hurt so much no more." He rolled over onto his hands and knees then slowly back onto his haunches and smiled. "Well look at that! Almost good as new!"

"Oh, hogwash!" Ida Mae marched up to Ryker, hands on hips, and shook a finger at him, a scowl on her face. "You are not as good as new and you know it! It's just lucky that you didn't get yourself and my David killed!"

Ryker blushed. "But…but…"

"No buts. Toby, you are now my patient. I am taking charge of you and I will give the orders around here as far as you are concerned." Ida Mae glanced at the others. "Did you all hear that?"

Subdued murmurs of "Yes ma'am," greeted her ears. Even Ryker said it.

"Good. First off, we're going to heat some water and give you a bath. Then we're going to put you to bed and send for Doc Swensen."

"Don't need Swensen. He –"

"We will send for Doctor Swensen," Ida Mae repeated, interrupting Ryker. "And starting tomorrow, you are going on a proper diet of greens and fruit and occasionally a SMALL portion of well-cooked meat."

"Greens and fruit! Sounds like you're sloppin' a hog!" Ryker said.

"I won't comment on that except to say that you were the one who said it," Ida Mae replied.

Jesse nudged David. "Boy, she wasn't whistling Dixie when she said she was taking charge." He filled a paper with tobacco and rolled a cigarette.

"Yup," David said. "I have a strong-willed wife here."

"You will also begin a program of exercise. You will go slowly at first, as much as Dr. Swensen and I feel you can tolerate, then build you up until we take a hundred pounds of lard off you," Ida Mae said.

"A-a hundred pounds!" Ryker gasped. "But Ida Mae, a prairie wind comes along, it'll plumb blow me away like tumbleweed."

"Not likely," Ida Mae answered.

"A hundred pounds!" Ryker looked at David pleadingly. "Talk to her, David."

"No chance," David said. "Once Ida Mae makes up her mind that you are her patient, the saints themselves can't dissuade her. I'm afraid you picked the wrong place to get sick if you just want to roll over and die. She won't let you."

"Oh, geez," Ryker whined. "Maybe I shouldn't have shot so straight at McQuiston after all."

The slap on his face from Ida Mae's hand surprised him more than it stung, for she did not hit him that hard. "I will not tolerate such foolish talk in front of my children," she said with a haughty air. "We do not condone talk of suicide here nor do we allow our patients to wallow in self pity. It is not conducive to improvement."

"Yes sir!" Ryker said, standing up unaided and saluting her. "My old friend Al Bodine who died in the civil war was a cavalry sergeant, and even he was gentler than you."

"Can you walk?" the sheriff said, surprised.

"Hurts like the blazes but yeah, I can make it to the house if I rest a bit first."

"All right then," Ida Mae said. "Matthew, head into town and summon Doc Swensen. David, you and I will guide Toby to the house lest he fall."

"Don't think I need Doc Swensen just now," Ryker said.

"I don't care what you think," Ida Mae said. "Matthew, get going."

As Matthew ran toward the barn, Jesse said, "Well, Ida Mae, David, I'll tote McQuiston on into town and wire Seth Bullock in Deadwood that his bounty hunter is dead. Doubt anyone will claim his body because it sounds like he has no next of kin, and he sure as the devil doesn't have any friends in Laramie who give a hoot about him. But maybe there are some relatives up Deadwood way, or a will or an estate or something like that. Bullock will know."

"What if it's a dead end?" David asked.

"Then we'll bury him on boot hill," the sheriff said. "He won enough money in that poker game to pay for his own funeral. We might even scare up a few mourners if I can talk the ladies auxiliary over to Our Saviour's Lutheran Church to serve a free lunch afterwards."

"Hilda and her friends at the church are decent about such things," Ida Mae said.

"Sheriff, check on that assault charge again' me, will you?" Ryker said. "That still bothers me." He motioned to Ida Mae. "That is, if it's okay with the Sarge here."

"I will."

"Adios then," David said, shaking Jesse's hand.

"Bye Jesse," Ida Mae added. "Thank you for everything."

"Yeah, thanks, sheriff," Ryker said. "Now David, would you help me inside the house lest we anger the sergeant here again?"

Four hours later, Matthew returned home with Dr. Magnus Swensen, M. D., Laramie's town physician. Ryker was resting comfortably in the guest bedroom after having had a hot bath and eaten a meal of beef and vegetable soup. Ida Mae cleaned his flesh wound and after Dr. Swensen examined it, he said he couldn't have cleaned it any better himself. He admonished the old man for going into the mountains on a hunting trip.

"You really are bound and determined to die aren't you, you stubborn old knothead!"

"Now Doc, we've been down this trail before."

David and Ida Mae entered the bedroom. "I got the elk butchered and the supplies put away," David said. "He's a nice one. Doc, take a roast back to town with you."

6

"Thanks, I will," Doc said. "It will taste great with onions simmered in."

"Doc, did you pass the sheriff on the road?" David asked.

"Nope, missed him."

"Well, he's got that bounty hunter McQuiston lying dead over the saddle of the horse he won off that cowboy at Kelly's Saloon."

"Mack Hanson, the one McQuiston slickered at cards and then killed in town," Doc said. "That killing is what put Jesse on McQuiston's trail out here to begin with. That and Angel LaRue, who filled him in on all the gory details. McQuiston was hunting Toby Ryker here, and the sheriff was hunting McQuiston."

"That's how it played out," David said.

Doc whistled. "Well, I'll be…what goes around comes around, I guess. As coroner, think I'll dissect that idiot McQuiston just for the heck of it. Scoop his guts up in my hands." He looked at Ryker and made a scooping motion with his hands while grinning wickedly.

"Doc, it's no wonder you have to practice medicine clear out here on the plains," Ryker said. "And I do mean *practice*. They won't let you in no decent sized town, you old quack."

"Well, when you croak, I won't bother to autopsy you," Doc retorted. "I know what you will die of and I'll just dull my knives cutting through all your blubber."

"What a charmer," Ryker huffed. "That's harder than I'd slam a door."

"If you two are done trading insults, I would like to discuss a recovery plan for Toby," Ida Mae said.

"Good idea," David said. "I've got chores to do and the late afternoon stage is due in fifteen minutes. I'll leave you three to your doctoring." So saying, he left and closed the door.

Doc stayed on for supper and that evening he discussed Ryker's medical condition with both Ida Mae and David. He was again amazed at the stamina of the old mountain man and the fact that throughout his ordeal in the mountains and the trip back to the ranch, he only needed to take eight nitroglycerin pills for his congestive heart failure. He left another prescription with Ida Mae, discussed her diet and weight loss plan with her, approved of it, and concluded by telling her if she ever considered going into medicine that she need look no further than his office in Laramie. He would gladly give her the money to get her medical degree if she would promise to share a practice with him for five years. Ida Mae thanked him but said she didn't think the territory was ready to accept a woman doctor. As the shadows were growing long, Doc then left the Stewart ranch and headed back to Laramie.

That night after Ryker and the kids were in bed, Ida Mae and David sat in the parlor and discussed the past few days. "I'm grateful we got Toby back here alive and survived that bounty hunter who was stalking us," David said. "That elk is just something extra as far as I'm concerned."

"Yes, it certainly could have ended differently," Ida Mae agreed. She poured them both another cup of coffee then sat next to him and kissed him. "You could have been killed up there, David. I try not to let myself think about that but whenever I do, I shiver inside."

"The way it played out, McQuiston got the drop on Jesse and rode into camp with him disguised as his prisoner," David said. "At that point, McQuiston was the only person armed. Toby figured that out right away and hid his pistol under his bedroll, but all my weapons were with the packs. It took me a while even with Jesse's help to figure out what was going on, and even then I still had to get to my rifle. Toby got in the first shot and then Jesse diverted McQuiston long enough for me to drop him with the Winchester." He sipped his coffee. "It wasn't pretty."

"Sounds like Toby saved your life up there," Ida Mae said.

"Yes he did, yet again." David took her hand. "Don't be too hard on him, dear. He's a lonely old man with nowhere to go who's scared of the dark and of what will happen to him next. He just doesn't want to admit it. He made out his will, Ida Mae. Left everything he has to us including a gold mine in Deadwood. Even gave his horse to Matthew. What do you think of that?"

Ida Mae said nothing, just smiled at David, kissed him again, and sipped her coffee too.

CHAPTER TWO

One year later, Toby Ryker was a changed man. Ida Mae Stewart made good on her promise and put him on a strict diet of greens and fruit as she said she would, and put him on and exercise program as well. Imperceptibly at first, the eventual transformation in Ryker was amazing to see. He dropped 85 pounds of body weight and toned up the underlying muscle on his still large frame. His posture improved and his wheezing ceased. He shed his buckskins that were now way too large for him in favor of store-bought clothing from the Barklay Emporium in Laramie. He kept his beard but shaved it close to his face and trimmed his hair back as well. He still carried the nitroglycerin pills from Doc Swensen but had not used them in months, for removing an inch of fat from over his heart improved its function considerably. And Ryker groused about it every waking second.

"Well, Sarge," he said as he entered the kitchen from his walk, "I ran from here to Denver and back in just over two hours carrying a hundred pound potato sack on my shoulders. What do you think of that?"

"Not too bad," Ida Mae replied. "But you still need to drop about fifteen more pounds. Tomorrow when you make that run, we'll try putting some weight in that sack. Maybe a potato or two."

Ryker opened his mouth to reply but no words came. He snorted and stomped off to the guest room.

"You're welcome," Ida Mae hollered after him.

"Mama, I'm having trouble figuring out the multiplication tables for the nines," Laura said from the parlor.

Ida Mae was working on a green tomato mincemeat pie when Laura called out. This time of year with the fall harvest upon them, she was doing a lot of canning for the winter months ahead along with home schooling her three children. Wiping her hands on her apron, she entered the parlor. "Laura, the nines are easy. When the first numeral goes up, the second numeral goes down. Here, I'll show you." She picked up the pencil and began to figure. "Start with nine times one, which is of course nine. Then nine times two, which is eighteen, see, one and eight. Then, nine times three, which is twenty-seven, see, the one goes up to a two and the eight comes down to a seven, then nine times four, which is thirty-six –"

"Oh, I get it, Laura said. "The two goes up to a three and the seven comes down to a six. This is easy, Mama."

"There's a formula to most ciphering," Ida Mae said. "Don't be afraid of numbers." She looked over Pauly's shoulder. "How is your script practice coming along, Pauly"

"Okay I guess, but these loops and swirls are kind of hard," Pauly replied.

"Let me see."

My name is Pauly James Stewart
I love my mother, Ida Mae Stewart.
I love my father, David Stewart.
I love my brother, Matthew Stewart.
I hate my sister, Laura Stewart. She is a big poop.
I love my mother

"Pauly!" Ida Mae said. "What you wrote about your sister is unchristian. Now apologize."

"I'm only kidding," Pauly whined.

"That is no way to kid! Now apologize!"

"What did he say, mama?" Laura asked, looking over Pauly's shoulder. "Pauly!" She slapped him on the head.

"Ouch! Well, you are a big poop!" He stuck his tongue out at her.

"Laura, sit down," Ida Mae said sternly. "Violence begets violence. Now Pauly, apologize. I'm waiting."

"Oh all right! I'm sorry, Laura."

"That's better," Ida Mae said. She crossed out Pauly's sentences about his sister and stood there while he wrote the line correctly five times. "Now keep at it, Pauly." She sighed and moved over to her eldest son. "Matthew, how about you?"

"I'm reading *Moby Dick*, mom," Matthew replied. "It's kind of scary."

"Maybe you shouldn't be reading that sensational literature." Ida Mae turned at the sound of hooves and a rumbling stage. "Anyway, the morning stage is here. Best go out and help your father switch teams."

"Okay mom," Matthew said. "That's way more fun anyway."

Ida Mae followed her eldest son as far as the front porch, glancing at the canning and seeing that the next batch had not boiled yet. She saw Ryker on the porch watching the Wells Fargo stagecoach as it pulled to a halt in the yard. He had a concerned look on his face as she approached him.

"Toby, is anything wrong?"

"It's that assault charge again' me in Deadwood, Ida Mae," Ryker said. "The last time we were in Laramie, the sheriff had word from Seth Bullock about it. It is still on the books up there and although I've tried, I can't get that out of my mind."

She was so used to Ryker calling her Sarge that when he referred to her by her given name, she knew he was very troubled. "Well, it isn't a serious charge anyway," Ida Mae said. "Dakota Territory won't come after you for it."

"I know, but it's still about me. It says I'm a criminal." He looked at her and blinked away a tear. "I ain't a criminal, Ida Mae. They don't understand what that matter was all about." His voice wavered as he said it.

Ida Mae patted Ryker on the shoulder and then returned to the kitchen as the old man looked out over the plain with a pained expression on his face.

Lefty Higgins jumped from the driver's seat of the stagecoach and ran to David. "Helen threw a shoe about a mile out."

"The right lead, huh? She split her hoof?" David asked.

"Naw, don't think so."

David moved quickly to the Percheron in harness on the right front side, leaned over, and grasped its foreleg firmly. The big draft horse mare raised her leg so the hoof could be examined. "I can replace the shoe all right. May have to shape it to her hoof in the forge a bit, but by tomorrow she'll be ready to pull."

"Good," Lefty said. "She's my best pacer. Say, you notice any strangers around lately?"

"No, can't say that I have," David replied. "Why?"

"There was a young fellow eyeballing us between here and Woods Landing this trip," Lefty said. "He looked to be alone but who can tell? I didn't like the looks of him."

"Probably just a tumbleweed passing through looking for work as a ranch hand," David said.

"Maybe," Lefty said. "He was smiley and all, but something about him didn't feel right."

"Well, tell Jesse about it when you get to Laramie," David said. "I'll keep my eyes open too."

That evening, Ida Mae talked to David about Ryker's obvious concern over the charge against him in Deadwood. They decided to head into Laramie the following day as they had other business to tend to there also. Only Matthew, who was quite proficient with the teams, would remain at the swing station to handle the switching of the coach horses.

The next morning, after a big breakfast for the Stewarts and oatmeal and toast for Ryker, the family bundled up and headed into town on the freight wagon. David and Matthew also loaded their excess produce into the back to sell to Jonas Barklay at the Emporium as they did every autumn after the harvest. It made for a full load but caused no strain for David's two powerful Percherons. They arrived in Laramie in about two hours' time.

"Ida Mae, why don't you and Toby go over to see Doc while the kids and I unload the produce at the Emporium," David suggested.

"That sounds fine," Ida Mae said. "We can have dinner at the Armbruster Hotel at noon."

"Okay," David said. "Toby, can you climb down by yourself?"

"Why sure, David," Ryker said. "Sarge has me so whipped into shape that I could probably beat her to Doc's in a foot race."

"Let's not push it," Ida Mae said as Laura and Pauly laughed. After she and Ryker climbed off the freight wagon, David clucked to the Percherons and they rumbled on down the street to Jonas Barklay's Emporium.

"Sarge, I want to duck into the bank here and draw some cash money from out of my account in Deadwood," Ryker said.

"Okay, I'll wait," Ida Mae said, pausing on the boardwalk and glancing up and down the street as she adjusted her gloves. A few minutes later Ryker returned and they resumed their walk to the doctor's office.

"Well if it isn't Ida Mae Stewart and Toby Ryker," Doc Swensen said, responding to the knock on his office door. "It is good to see you again. It's been a couple months."

"Likewise, Doctor Swensen," said Ida Mae. "Do you have a few minutes for Toby and me?"

"Yeah, the Sarge here wants you to check me over," Ryker said, forcing himself to sound peeved.

"Sure, I have the time. Come on in," Doc said, closing the door behind them. "Toby, turn around. Let me have a look at you."

"Geez," Ryker grumped. "Like inspecting a hanging side of beef."

"Oh, hush up!" Doc said, walking around Ryker and eyeing him from head to foot. He put his stethoscope to his ears and listened all over Ryker's chest for several moments then likewise his back, then checked his pulse against the second hand on his timepiece. "Sit down here on the examining table." When Ryker complied, Doc grabbed a tongue depressor. "Now, open your mouth and say 'ah'."

"Oh for cripes sake!"

"Shut up! No, I mean open your mouth like I said."

"Ah."

"No sign of thrush." Doc tossed the tongue depressor. "I wonder what that thing is hanging down from the top of your throat." He winked at Ida Mae.

"You old quack!"

"Toby, how much weight have you lost?"

"You have to ask the Sarge that," Ryker replied. "She keeps track of all that stuff."

"He is down eighty-five pounds since we started a year ago," Ida Mae said.

"Eighty-five pounds!" Doc swiped his hand across his mouth. "Well, I declare. Ida Mae, if I hadn't seen it with my own eyes, I wouldn't have believed it. A year ago I wouldn't have bet five cents that this old Jasper would have lasted the winter, what with his heart trouble and the risk of infection from the gunshot and all, and now here he is almost good as new. His heart is steady and his color is good. It's amazing, Ida Mae. Just amazing."

"There's another part too," Ryker said, beaming.

"Oh?" Doc said. What is that?"

"Would you excuse us a second, Sarge?"

"Sure," Ida Mae replied, turning and looking out the window.

"Let's go in your sick room. Is it empty?" Ryker asked.

"At the moment," Doc said.

"That's all this will take," Toby replied as the two men entered the small hospital ward and closed the door. "Little Toby's been making an appearance lately too.

"Little Toby?"

"Yeah, little Toby, my carrot. Started a couple months ago. For the first time in years it stands up in the mornin'." Ryker grinned from ear to ear as he said it.

"That is a side benefit of improved circulation," Doc said. "Congratulations. If you want it to do more than stand up and would like to see it salute, stop over to Kelly's and see Angel. She's clean."

"With my heart and all, you mean...."

"I think it would be all right."

"Say, how do you know so much about this Angel girl anyhow?" Ryker said, nudging Doc and grinning.

"Never mind how I know," Doc said. "I just know, that's all."

Doc tugged at his ear as he and Ryker returned to the outer office. "Ida Mae, I do believe it may be beneficial to add a glass of wine to Toby's menu on a daily basis. It is a good blood thinner."

Ryker licked his lips and smiled. "Eight or ten glasses will thin it even better."

"No!" Both Doc and Ida Mae shouted in unison.

"One glass a day, that is all," Doc added.

"No harm in trying," Ryker said.

"Doc, what do we owe you?" Ida Mae said.

"Not we, me, Sarge," Ryker said, digging out his money pouch. "It's me he stuck his scope on, not you."

"How does ten dollars cash money for the exam and a new prescription sound?" Doc said.

"Sounds fair to me," Ryker replied, handing over a ten dollar gold piece. "Don't want to have any bills. Well Doc, me and Sarge here best head on over to Kelly's to get some of that medicine you prescribed."

"Toby, you go on," Ida Mae said. "I don't approve of entering those establishments but I trust you know your way around them. I'll finish up here and meet you at the Armbruster for dinner at noon."

"As you wish, Sarge," Ryker said.

"I'll give Ida Mae another prescription for you just to have on hand," Doc said.

"Okay." Ryker headed out the door, pulling it shut behind him.

"Doc," Ida Mae said when they were alone, "is Toby in good enough condition to travel?"

"Do you mean on a long trip?" Doc asked.

"Yes, to Deadwood," Ida Mae replied.

"That is a fair trek," Doc said. "Well, I guess it wouldn't hurt if he went by train. But he shouldn't try and make that trip by horseback any more. What do you have in mind?"

"I'm not sure I have anything in mind just yet," Ida Mae said. "At this point I'm just checking on possibilities." She arose and donned her gloves. "Doc, it was nice seeing you again."

"The pleasure was all mine," Doc Swensen said, escorting her to the door. "Oh, here are some more nitroglycerin pills." He poured a quantity into a vial. "Although I doubt he will need them right away at least. You've worked wonders, Ida Mae. My hat is off to you."

"He complains about it a lot."

"Toby Ryker probably complained the day he was born," Doc said. "That's just him. Think nothing of it. He appreciates you, Ida Mae."

"I hope so," Ida Mae said, departing.

"Hi, Kelly, ain't seen you in a spell," Ryker said, walking into the saloon. I need a couple gallons of table wine."

Just Kelly and Angela "Angel" LaRue were working the place this time of the day. Except for one old man at the bar who was drunk and snoozing, the place was empty.

"Sure thing," Kelly said. "Got some in the store room. You like it sweet or dry?"

"Sweet, I reckon," Ryker said. "And speaking of sweet, what a sweet young thing you are, ma'am."

"Thanks," Angel said. "You're kind of sweet yourself. You're Toby Ryker, aren't you?"

"Yeah, how'd you know?"

"I heard tell you got the first slug in John McQuiston last year before David Stewart blew his heart out with that big Winchester of his," she said. "I did a little dance when the sheriff came into town with him draped over a saddle."

"Recollect him mentioning you after the shootout," Ryker said. "He was a wicked one, he was."

"He was a low-down crazy devil," Angel snarled. "Meaner than a rabid wolf. I'll give you a poke for free just for helping rid the world of him."

Ryker looked around. "A free poke, huh? How much time you got?"

Angel looked at the clock. "How's a half hour sound?"

"That's more than enough," Ryker grabbed Angel's hand and headed toward the stairs. "Okay, Kelly?"

Kelly nodded, so after they got to the bedroom, Ryker said, "Angel, I don't need a poke, but I said that to get you up here away from Kelly. I ain't played a game of checkers with a pretty young thing in ages. You got a board?"

As they played, Angel told Ryker how McQuiston promised her they would leave town and maybe go to California. She had been stuck in Laramie nearly two years now and was tired of it. But she was trapped; she had no funds to move on. Being a soft touch, Ryker felt sorry for the young woman.

"Angel, here," he said, reaching into his money pouch. "Here's two hundred and fifty dollars in gold. It will take you to California or wherever you want to go and get you a grubstake."

Angel looked at the money, stunned. "Toby, I don't expect you to do this."

"And I didn't expect you to offer an old yahoo like me a free poke either," Ryker said. "Let's just say I see more possibilities for you than growing old here in a Laramie saloon. You can go to California, San Francisco maybe, and woo one of those big bankers or railroad men, get married, and settle down right proper like. You got class, Angel. Don't never let anybody tell you different."

Moving over to Ryker, Angel wiped a tear from her eye and kissed him. "You are a kind, gentle man. We girls don't see many of your kind in here. Now I'm going to show you my appreciation." She ran her tongue over her lips while staring provocatively into his eyes and then moved her checker directly into the path of his, allowing him to make three jumps.

"King me," Ryker said, grinning.

At twenty minutes to twelve they were finished. Ryker stopped at the bedroom door and kissed Angel tenderly. "Angel, this is the most pleasant half hour I've spent with a lady in years, and I mean that sincerely. Post me a card when you get to California. I'll be here, and if you need more money to start a business, maybe open a dress shop or something, just tell me. I'll set you up proper."

"You can count on that," Angel said, following him out into the saloon.

"Angel, draw a beer for that fellow at the bar," Kelly hollered. "Toby, your wine is ready. That'll be four dollars."

"Thanks Kelly," Ryker hollered back. I'll pay the angel here."

"No you won't," she said, pushing his money away. "You've paid enough. I'll take care of it." Angel hollered back to Kelly. "It's paid for, and I'll and serve the beer." She whispered to Ryker, "I'll tell him later that this is my last day, thanks to you."

"Kelly will probably never forgive me. Follow your dream, girl." He looked at the clock again. "Just enough time to run a couple errands and meet up with the Stewarts for dinner. Good luck, Angel." He nodded to her, picked up the wine, and left the saloon.

At twelve o'clock noon Ryker entered the dining room of the Armbruster Hotel and rejoined the Stewart family. He sampled a glass of wine and enjoyed a small portion of roast chicken.

"Jonas Barklay paid $48.43 cash money for the garden goods," David said. "You earned that, Ida Mae."

"Laura and Pauly helped," Ida Mae said. "After dinner I want to go over to the bank and open a savings account for the children. We'll put ten dollars in each and the rest of it in our general account."

"Sounds fair to me," David said. "But, I think my hard-working wife and kids deserve to spend some on themselves at the Emporium before we go home today too."

"I agree, David," Ryker said. "Sarge and the little soldiers deserve a treat."

After dinner, the group returned to the Emporium where Ida Mae purchased a bolt of fancy cloth and Laura and Pauly got a few toys and some candy to take back to the ranch. After paying for the goods they went over to the bank to open accounts for the children as Ida Mae had suggested. That done, they deposited the balance in their general account. David looked then looked again, stunned, at their balance. A thousand dollars had been added to their account that day. He looked at Ida Mae questioningly, showing her the balance, and then at Ryker. Hands in his pockets, Ryker glanced at the ceiling and pretended to whistle then winked at David and Ida Mae and the kids and grinned.

"Toby?" David said. "What do you know about this?"

"Quite a bit," Ryker said. "You folks put me up for the last year, fed me, watered me, done my laundry, tended to me, walked off my flab, and didn't charge me even one large penny. That ain't right. If I'd gone to one of those fancy mineral springs places, it would have cost me a small fortune to get done what you did out of the goodness of your hearts. In fact, if it wasn't for you, I'd be dead by now, plain and simple. I can afford to do this and I want to do this. In a small way, it's a thank you for all you did for me."

Both David and Ida Mae were speechless for a moment. Ida Mae regained her senses first. "Toby, you don't have to do this."

"She's right," David agreed.

"I know I don't, and I know if I was poor, you'd still have done it for me and that's heart-warming," Ryker said. "But I ain't poor, I can afford to pay my way and I want to do this. I'm sure the money will come in handy for you somehow. Besides that, there was a post for me at the telegraph office. They had it for weeks. My gold mine in Deadwood, my partner struck new veins! My share's worth near twenty-three thousand now."

"Twenty-three thousand dollars! Toby, you're rich!" David said, laughing. "Thank you for the money. We'll find a use for it."

"Yes, thank you Toby," Ida Mae said.

"You're plumb welcome," Ryker said. "But that don't mean I'm going to quit calling you Sarge or that I'm going to quit complaining about everything you do."

"I should hope not," Ida Mae said. "I've gotten used to it. If you stopped now, I wouldn't know how to act."

The entire family shared a chuckle with Ryker as they left the bank, climbed into the freight wagon, and headed out of town toward the swing station.

Deadwood Days

CHAPTER THREE

Arriving back at the swing station by mid-afternoon, Ryker and the Stewarts were soon into their daily routine again. The old man stood on the porch and stretched then sat in the rocking chair. He had just gotten comfortable when Ida Mae stuck her head out the door.

"And just what do you think you're doing?"

"Nothin' Sarge, just takin' it easy."

"Aren't you forgetting something?"

"Oh? And what might that be, pray tell?"

"Just because we went into town today doesn't mean you don't need to get your exercise. Go on. Get up and start walking. I don't want to see you back here for another hour."

"Another hour? Sarge, I already got my exercise today."

"What do you mean?"

Not wanting to tell her about Angel and his vigorous checker games, Ryker arose from the rocking chair. "Never mind, I'll go. Geez, I never get a break. Even after I keel over, you'll probably put a shovel in my hand and make me dig my own grave."

"There's a thought," Ida Mae said, returning to the house.

Ryker grabbed his coat as a brisk breeze had come up then headed out to the Woods Landing road. He had developed two routes for himself, one going east and one going west, and knew just how far to go in each direction to satisfy Ida Mae that he was getting enough exercise.

When he got to the end of the trail into the yard he flipped a coin, which determined for him that today he would take the west walk. He had gone a half hour in that direction when he stopped, bent over, touched his toes, and then surveyed the surrounding countryside. He was about to start back for the house again when the hint of gunmetal reflecting off the sun caught his eye. Looking at it closely, he saw a man and a horse under some trees down by the Big Laramie River. The man was playing with his nickel-plated revolver, twirling it, and that was the reflection he saw. When the man noticed Ryker looking at him, he picked up the reins to the horse and started walking toward him.

"Howdy, old-timer," the young man said. He was pleasant looking with dark hair, was sort of husky built, and had blue eyes that twinkled. If he were back in his scrapping days, Ryker figured this chap would be fun to wrestle with and maybe beat the crap out of.

"Howdy yourself," Ryker replied. "You twirl that .45 real nice. Can you hit anything with it?"

"If it isn't too far away and if I throw it straight enough," the fellow said. "I don't cotton to shooting at people though. Most of them can shoot back."

"Where you headed and who are you?" Ryker asked, chuckling.

"Everywhere and nowhere. Name's Bobby Parker, but folks just calls me Butch."

"And I'm Toby Ryker, the biggest, meanest, orneriest, ugliest hombre between here and the Wells Fargo swing station, which is where I'm headed. Want to mosey along?"

"Sure. I ain't got anything better to do, but I sure am getting hungry. Ain't et in a day. Run out of beans." His stomach started to growl. "You got any vittles on you?"

"Afraid not," Ryker said. "Sarge, ah, Ida Mae Stewart, she's tending me since I've been ailing, she wouldn't hear of me sneaking vittles on the side." He patted his belly. "A year ago there was eighty-five more pounds sitting here."

"Eighty-five pounds? Wow! You still look big to me."

"Well, I was toting eighty-five more and it nearly killed me. Anyway, come on to the swing station with me. Ida Mae, why, she's the best cook between here and Santa Fe. She'll put some meat on your bones."

"I don't mind working for my keep," Bobby Parker replied as the two men started walking east on the Woods Landing road. When they got to the swing station, Ida Mae graciously invited the stranger into the house for supper. Even though they had been in town much of the day, she had a big kettle of beef stew left over and told Bobby that stew always tasted better the second time around after it had a chance to cook down.

Bobby said little at the table at first but ate ravenously. It was obvious he was half starved. Once he was well fed, he settled back, relaxed, and took out a sack of tobacco.

"We do not smoke at the dinner table, Mister Parker," Ida Mae said. "You are most welcome to smoke, but please do it either in the parlor or outside."

"That's right Butch," David quipped. "I'm the head of the house and Ida Mae would even whup me if I tried to smoke at the table. Tried it just once and she came at me with a carving knife. Left me with a six inch scar across my chest."

Bobby Parker gulped. "Gee whiz, you folks play rough."

"Oh, don't pay any attention to David," Ida Mae said. "He's just talking to hear his head rattle." She took a last bite of stew then set her fork on her plate and touched her napkin to her lips. "Besides, I doubt that scar is more than three inches long."

Bobby Parker laughed. "I'll smoke outside ma'am, if you'll excuse me." He winked at Matthew, stood up, tousled Pauly's hair, and smiled at Laura.

"He's cute, Mama," Laura said after Bobby stepped outside.

Yes, he's a handsome boy," Ida Mae agreed.

"Laura's got a boy-friend," Pauly sing-songed the words.

"Shut up, you little brat!" Laura said, slapping Pauly on the leg.

"Ouch! You big nincompoop!" Pauly retorted, punching Laura on the arm.

"Children!" Ida Mae said.

"Yes, Laura, Pauly, if you want to duke it out, we'll schedule a wrestling match, put up a ring, and sell tickets," David said. "We might as well make some money off of you two acting stupid."

"Maybe I shouldn't have invited him here," Ryker said.

"No, it's not that," Ida Mae said. "It's these two monkeys we claim as our own that are the problem. Now Laura, apologize to Pauly."

"Do I have to, Mama?" Laura whined. "He started it."

"Yes, you have to," Ida Mae said. "Now, apologize."

Laura paused a moment. "I'm so truly, deeply sorry, Pauly," she whispered, pooching up her lips and making a kissing motion at him.

"Such sincerity; no need to overdo it, Laura," Ida Mae said.

"Sorry too," Pauly said hurriedly. "Mama, I'm done now. Can I go out and play?"

"No, you and Laura do up the dishes first. Then, you can go out and play for a bit, but just remember that tonight is bath night."

"Reckon I'll mosey out to the barn and check on the stock for the night," David said. Toby, Matthew, you coming?"

"Yup, right behind you Pa," Matthew said.

"Me too David," Ryker said. As he passed Ida Mae he added, "Right tasty stew, Sarge. Not as good as oatmeal, but right tasty."

Bobby Parker accompanied David, Ryker, and Matthew to the barn and pitched in with the chores. While so engaged he told David he had ridden past the Buckley ranch up the road where all the longhorn cattle were. This struck David as odd because Sam Buckley was one of the few ranchers in the area that raised those newfangled shorthorn Hereford beef cattle instead of longhorns. Bobby was obviously not a cattleman. Either that or he was an outright liar about riding past the Buckley ranch.

David told him if he didn't mind sleeping on the cot he had in the small office next to the tack room, he could offer the young man a week's work at three dollars a day plus keep. Bobby Parker fairly jumped at the chance, and over the next week proved to be a willing and able worker. He was also good with horses and knew how to harness, shoe, and use a rope. At the end of the week he bid Ryker and the Stewarts farewell, took his 21 dollars, mounted up, and rode out of their lives just as quickly as he had ridden into them. Although they didn't know it then, they would cross paths with him again.

A couple weeks after the trip into Laramie, Ida Mae and David spent some time alone in the parlor late one evening after everyone else was in bed. Ida Mae had been turning some things over in her mind and it was time to talk to David about it.

"David?"

"Hmm?" said David, looking up from the *Farmer's Almanac* and pushing his reading glasses up onto his forehead.

"I've been thinking a lot about Toby lately. What would you think about going to Deadwood and helping him clear his name up there? I believe it weighs heavily on his mind."

Reaching for his pipe, David packed with it with tobacco and lit up. "I think you are right, Ida Mae. I think that has plagued Toby ever since he found out about it."

"He doesn't talk much about it," Ida Mae added. "But when he does, you can tell it really bothers him."

"Great minds travel in the same circles," he said, grinning. "I've been giving that some thought too. Toby has given us the deed to that gold mine in Deadwood and it is producing handsomely. It will continue to do so for some time to come, and Toby's partner is of an age with Toby and also wants to retire. The other fellow who he calls Stumpy just works it, so it's ours free and clear." He smiled at her. "I suspect they could also use a good schoolmarm in Deadwood. The problem is this place. What do we do with it?"

"I suppose we could always put it up for sale," Ida Mae said.

"This is a good, fertile ranch and the swing station brings in a steady income. It probably wouldn't be that hard to sell," David said. "But Ida Mae, tell me this, do you really want to leave? After all, we built this place from nothing. We have fourteen years of our sweat invested here. Are you willing to give it all up and run off to somewhere that we will have to start all over?"

"I've thought about that too," Ida Mae said. "Yes, we have put a lot of our lives and a lot of hard work into this ranch and made it our home. All of our children and the baby who died are rooted here. And I'm not going to pretend that I won't miss it because I know that I will. But on the other hand, I have you and the children, and I home school them anyway so they will get educated no matter where we are. Matthew is nearly of age and there is an opportunity knocking in Deadwood right now that surpasses anything we could ever hope to gain here. And all that is in addition to helping Toby clear his name." She nodded at him. "I think we should do it. I think this spring we should put this place up for sale and take the train to Deadwood." She stood and approached him. "It will be kind of exciting to go out and seek our fame and fortune just like the forty-niners did."

"I always wondered why folks called them the forty-niners," David said, winking at Ida Mae.

"Do you think it could be because they struck gold at Sutter's Mill back in eighteen forty-nine?" Ida Mae said, playing it straight.

"By jingo, I think you may have something there," David replied. He leaned up and kissed her. "You're quite a woman, Ida Mae."

"I won't argue that," she said. "But back to the subject, such a move as we are contemplating will impact more lives than just yours and mine. I think it's time we call a family meeting."

"Couldn't agree more," David said, knocking the ash out of his pipe. "Woman of mine, let's go to bed." He hugged her. "I'm so lucky I let you catch me."

"Catch you? That's not how I remember our courtship."

"Oh? Is your mind starting to slip already?"

"David, you always did have a vivid imagination."

"Let's go to bed."

"As Toby would say, okay Sarge."

The next day passed quickly and uneventfully, filled with the normal busy routine of a working homestead. During supper, David announced that after the meal there would be a family powwow in the parlor with the presence of all family members required.

"How about me, David?" Ryker asked.

"Toby, after all this time you shouldn't have to ask," David replied. "Yes, you are certainly a part of this family."

"Okay, see, Pauly and I were going to walk over to Tie Siding as a bonus walk, but since this come up, we'll put it off until another time." Ryker winked at Pauly.

"Yeth," Pauly said. He had just lost a front tooth that afternoon so was forced to bear the indignity of speaking with a lisp for a short time. "Thun of a bitth, I hate thith," he added.

"Pauly James Stewart!" said Ida Mae. "We do not use such language in this house! Young man, here is a knife. March outside right now to the orchard. Cut a nice thick switch and bring it back here. You are going to get a licking!"

"Oh Mama, pleath, I'm tho thorry, don't make me do thith." He started to cry.

"Pauly," Ida Mae pointed to the door, "now!"

26

Looking around at all the others at the table, Pauly saw them staring back at him. Ryker had sympathy in his eyes. David tried to hide his amusement as did Matthew. Laura stuck out her tongue at him.

"Laura," Ida Mae cautioned, "you aren't too old to cut a switch either. Stay out of this."

"Yes Mama," said Laura, eyes downcast.

Crying all the way, Pauly took the knife from Ida Mae and went out to the orchard. He cut what he thought was a decent sized switch and returned to the house with it. By the time he arrived at the kitchen, all the others had finished eating and, except for Ida Mae, adjourned to the parlor.

"Now Pauly, give me that knife and that switch," Ida Mae ordered.

"Yeth Mama," Pauly whimpered.

"Bend over this chair."

Pauly, still whimpering, did as ordered. Ida Mae put her hand over Pauly's behind and hit it several whacks with the switch, which made a loud slapping sound. The only part of the switch that came into contact with Pauly was the very tip, which stung his legs a bit, but to hear him yowl, one would think he was being beaten to death.

"Now Pauly, what has this taught you?" Ida Mae said, straightening her youngest up from over the chair.

"Never to thwear in front of you," Pauly sobbed.

"Never to swear period," Ida Mae corrected him. "Where did you hear such language? We don't talk that way around here."

"From Butth. When he thed it, it didn't thound tho bad."

"Butch? You mean, Bobby Parker?"

"Yeth."

"I might have known," Ida Mae said. "Now go into the parlor with the others."

"Yeth, Mama." He entered the parlor and sat alone, ashamed to look at the rest of the family.

Ida Mae composed herself and entered a few moments later. She sat next to David and both of them looked at the family. "We need to discuss something with you kids," David began. "Your mother and I have been thinking about putting the ranch up for sale and moving to Deadwood up north in Dakota Territory. You don't know this, but Toby, kind man that he is, has left us ownership in a working gold mine up there on a place they call Potato Creek."

"That's a fact, kids," Ryker said. "Your folks and I jawed about this some today and I agree with everything they are saying."

"It is producing a lot of gold and will continue to do so for quite some time," David continued. "At today's gold prices, that inheritance is very valuable. The problem up there is that Toby is in no condition to run the mine and his partner also wishes to retire. They need someone to manage it for them. Toby has offered that job to me."

"Oh Papa, this so wonderful," Laura said.

"This is real nice of you Mister Ryker," Matthew said.

"Well shucks, I'm just one of those nice old retired mountain men you hear about these days." Ryker chuckled.

"What about you, Mama?" Pauly ventured to ask. "Do you want to move? What will you do?"

"I think I'll go back to teaching like I did when I first moved out here to Laramie with your Grandpa Sebastian and Grandma Hannah and Uncle George," Ida Mae said. "I have kept up my credentials and I bet they need school teachers there. I could start a home school for the children of Deadwood."

"I'll mith it here," Pauly ventured to say. "Thith ith home."

"Home is wherever we are as a family," Ida Mae said.

"That's right kids," David agreed. "As long as we are together, wherever we are will be our home."

"I just said that," Ida Mae teased.

"Not as well as I did," David teased back. "The only difference is that we will live in the town of Deadwood instead of out on a ranch."

"Mama, I like that idea," Laura said. "Sure, this is the only home I've ever known because I was born here. But to be honest with you, I get lonesome living way out here by ourselves with nobody but..." she tapped Pauly on the head, "THITH guy to play with." She giggled as Pauly slapped her hand away.

"I can understand that," Ida Mae said. "It is important for children, and grownups too for that matter, to live close to others their ages. It helps them grow up and learn good manners."

"And itth more fun, too," Pauly said. "I'll mith Elithabeth Buckley, though."

"You can become pen pals," Ida Mae said. "And you will meet new friends, Pauly."

"Well, what do you think?" David said, lighting up his pipe. "Should we put this ranch up for sale come spring?"

"Yes, let's do it!" Matthew replied.

"This will be so exciting," Laura said, clapping her hands.

"I geth tho," Pauly said.

"Now you're a-talking, kids," Ryker said. "And remember, I spent some time in Deadwood so I know some folks there. We won't be strangers."

"Do you know any children up there?" Laura said.

"Can't honestly say I do," Ryker replied. "Whores and drunks mostly. There's this one old heifer, Poker Alice, she –"

"Well, there are plenty of fine folks in Deadwood," Ida Mae interrupted. "It is a relatively new town that is full of optimism for the future, and we are going to be a part of that future."

"Your mother is right," David replied. "This is our chance to get in on the ground floor of not only a new town and new industry, but also a new way of life. I want that for Ida Mae and me, but for you children as well."

"But Matthew, Laura, Pauly, there's something else you should know," Ryker said. "Your pa and ma know about this and it's only right you know about it too. There's another reason to go to Deadwood." He pulled a folded poster from his pocket and opened it, revealing his image. "It's this. I took it off that bounty hunter your pa shot winter before last when we went hunting. We never told you, but that bounty hunter was hunting something too. He was hunting me." He passed the poster to the children.

"This says you murdered someone," Matthew said.

"Did you kill somebody, Mister Ryker?" Laura asked.

Pauly said nothing, just stared at the poster then back at Ryker.

"Yeah, I killed some people in my time, but I didn't kill this feller they're talking about here," Ryker said. "Sheriff O'Brian cleared that up for me. But I did shoot him and they still have an assault charge again' me up there. That's another reason we want to go to Deadwood."

"Why did you thoot him?" Pauly said. "He make you mad?"

"He did more than that, Pauly. Even now after all these years, it's still hard for me to say it. See kids, I had a family once too, an Indian one, a wife and daughter. My wife's name was Wild Flower and my daughter's name was Hope. They were Pawnee and this man I shot…" Ryker began to choke up so David and Ida Mae moved to his side to comfort him.

"Thanks, David, Ida Mae, but the kids have the right to hear this through. This man I shot, he and a bunch of other buffalo hunters killed my wife and daughter in the Indian village where we lived. That's why I shot him. Would have killed him too, and if I had, then my face on this poster would be deserved. But I didn't kill him. A little girl even younger than you, Pauly, came out and begged me not to. Said he was her papa and begged for his life so I let him live. It wasn't until I moved here that I found out he was ailing. He had the consumption or something and up and died anyway. That's when they stuck my face on this piece of paper and that's when that bounty hunter came a-looking for me. You know most of the rest. What you don't know is that they still have an assault charge again' me in Deadwood because I shot that man. That means they think I am a criminal." Ryker looked gravely at all three children. "I'm not a criminal. Was justified in shooting that man and want the chance to prove it to the folks in Deadwood."

"Listening to you tell it again Toby, I think you are going to need a lawyer," David said.

"Yes, you are probably right," Ryker agreed, "or somebody who knows something about the law anyway. Maybe Bullock can help me there."

"So, children," Ida Mae said, "this will be a chance for a new life for us, but it will also be a chance for Toby to bring peace to his life. And remember, Deadwood is still a gold camp. It is a wild town and there is danger there. It is not a civilized city like the ones back East. We will have to be careful."

Laura and Pauly approached Ryker, one on either side. "Mister Ryker, if somebody came to the ranch and killed Mama and me, I would hope that Papa would kill him back," Laura said.

"Yeth, I'd even kill him back," Pauly said.

Ida Mae thought about launching into a lecture about the folly of an eye for an eye and a tooth for a tooth, but she checked herself and said nothing.

"And even though your mama's done a heap good job of tending me, the simple fact is that I ain't getting any younger," Ryker said.

"Sooner or later, I will die. It happens to everybody and it'll happen to me too."

Laura began to cry. "I don't want you to die, Grandpa Ryker."

"Me neithow, Gwandpa," Pauly added, also shedding a tear. It was the first time either child had referred to the old man as a grandfather.

"Oh, Laura, Pauly," Ryker said, hugging them both, "don't cry. It's plumb natural and I'm ready for it. And by the way, proud I am to have you call me your grandpa. Please don't stop."

Ida Mae and David had fallen silent as the old man spoke. "I don't think that will occur yet for some time yet, Toby," Ida Mae said softly.

"I'm inclined to agree with her," David said.

"Hope you're right," Ryker said, "because it is important to me to clear my name with the law first."

David arose and hugged the old man. "That will be our priority."

"It's settled then," Ryker said after hugging back. "I'll get off a wire to my partner and tell him to expect us come spring."

"Just as soon as this place is sold," David said.

"Just as soon as it sells," Ryker agreed. "And that won't take long."

CHAPTER FOUR

Ryker's words proved prophetic, for in May of 1887, it seemed David Stewart just mentioned to a few folks that the ranch was for sale and interested buyers began to show up. The Stewarts ended up selling to Sam Buckley, their neighbor on the Woods Landing road. He already homesteaded a thousand acres but with three sons was eager to add another thousand to his holdings. All too soon, the day to depart for Deadwood arrived.

"David, I wish you and the family the best up there Dakota way," Sam said. He and his family rode over to the ranch to see the Stewarts on their way.

"Thank you Sam," David replied. "I hope you enjoy this place as much as we did."

"I'm sure we will," Sam replied. "Plan to move the family over here. This house has more room than ours, and with the Wells Fargo contract, I need to be here, anyway."

"Caleb, Dexter, and Joshua will be a big help to you," David said, nodding to the three Buckley boys who were visiting with Matthew and Laura in the yard.

"That they will," Sam replied. "They know how to harness and tend to the teams so that will be their job. I'll concentrate on building up the Hereford cattle herd."

"With the railhead so close and the eastern markets for beef, you'll do just fine," David said.

"Good Lord willing," Sam replied.

Ryker, Ida Mae, and Cecilia Buckley joined the men from the house where Ida Mae had given the Buckley woman a tour and showed her the ins and outs of her new home. "Well, we're all packed and set to go," Ryker said, the sound of excitement in his voice.

"Thank you for helping us tote our goods to the railhead today, Sam," Ida Mae said.

"My pleasure," Sam replied. "We will miss you folks."

"Yes," Cecilia said. "You have been good neighbors."

"As have you," David replied.

The adults shook hands and embraced. "Matthew, Laura, Pauly, come along now," David said. "It's time to go."

Pauly was uncharacteristically quiet today. Most of the time he spent with Elizabeth Buckley who was his same age, walking around the Stewart yard and pointing out things. At his father's voice, he handed her a small box wrapped with a bow. "This is for you," he said. "I'll miss you, Elizabeth. I'll post you my address when I know what it is. Write to me, okay?"

Elizabeth opened the box to find a small locket engraved "E" and "P" inside that Pauly had bought at the Emporium in Laramie. She looked at him. "But I didn't get you anything."

"You didn't have to," Pauly said. "I wanted to do this."

"This is very nice of you Pauly," Elizabeth said, putting the chain around her neck. "Yes, I will write to you."

Once the Stewarts and Ryker were aboard the buckboard, they paused a moment and took one last look around the place they called home for better than fifteen years.

"Nurture it Sam," David said.

"It will reward you handsomely," Ida Mae added.

"I'm sure of it," Sam said. He mounted the freight wagon loaded with goods which stood next to the buckboard, signaled to Caleb and Dexter, his two eldest sons, to hop onboard, and both rigs rumbled off toward the Woods Landing road and the town of Laramie beyond. Pauly, sitting on the rear of the buckboard, looked back at Elizabeth Buckley until a bend in the road hid her from view.

Upon their arrival in Laramie, the group went directly to the Union Pacific Depot. There, they loaded the trunks and housewares onto a depot cart that was then taken to a freight car and packed away. David's Percheron team and the buckboard would also make the trip to Deadwood aboard different cars. The team was penned and fed for the night and would be loaded the following morning just prior to departure. Ryker's horse Wino, now belonging to Matthew Stewart, and a riding horse belonging to David were both tied behind the freight wagon and would also make the journey to Deadwood. These tasks completed, the family purchased their tickets at the depot and after bidding Sam and his sons farewell, they walked to the hotel to spend the night.

The next morning after breakfast in the dining room, the Stewarts returned to the depot and boarded the train. Shortly thereafter the conductor shouted "Board!" on the platform outside their window. Then the whistle blew and the chug-chug sound of the steam engine reached their ears, and when the Stewarts felt the passenger car beginning to move under them, they knew their adventure was underway.

"Mama, are we there yet?" Pauly said about ten minutes into the ride.

"No Pauly, we won't be there for a few days," Ida Mae said.

"Pauly, how dumb are you?" Laura said.

"Shut up! Mama, Laura said I'm dumb."

"Children, this will be a long trip," Ida Mae said. "Let's make it a pleasant one by being agreeable and by not picking at one another."

"That's right," David said sternly. "I'll not have you performing on this train. You can sit with the horses if you want to act like animals."

"David, they're just being anxious," Ryker said.

"We all are," David said. "That's no excuse for snapping at one another."

"Guess you're right," Ryker said, standing. "Think I'll walk a bit and stretch my legs."

"I'll go with you," Matthew said.

"Okay, Matthew," Ryker replied. "I welcome your company. We can stop in the dining car and I'll buy you a sarsaparilla."

35

As they prepared to walk up the aisle, a stern looking man walked toward them. He was dressed in a suit. They saw he was armed. He eyed them suspiciously but said nothing, continuing through the car and into the next one.

"Looked like a lawman," Ryker said to David.

"Pinkerton," David replied. "My guess is they're transporting some gold this trip."

"Never thought of that. Might be dropping off a payroll shipment at Fort Laramie."

When the train arrived at Fort Laramie, Ryker was proven correct. Several cavalry troopers and a freight wagon greeted the train. The Stewarts watched as two strongboxes were loaded onto the wagon, overseen by the same man who had passed through their coach earlier.

The train was soon on the move again and out onto open plain, moving along at a brisk pace of 38 miles per hour. Laura and Pauly watched out the window for a time, but after a half hour, lulled by the clickity-clack of the iron wheels on the rails and the gentle rocking motion of the passenger car, they soon dozed off. David read a copy of the newspaper he picked up at the station in Laramie and Ida Mae tried to concentrate on a copy of the *Harpers Weekly Journal of Civilization*. It was difficult for her to do so however, because the motion of the train and the smell of the smoke from the engine stack made her slightly nauseous. As for Toby and Matthew, they returned from the dining car and had just joined the two younger Stewarts in a short siesta when the train suddenly came to a halt out in the middle of nowhere.

Instantly awake, they noticed horsemen riding past their window. David and Toby checked their weapons. "Ida Mae, kids, you stay put," David said. "This looks like a holdup."

"A holdup!" Ida Mae said. "What do they want?"

"Maybe our cash money," David said. "I don't know what else is on the train."

Gunshots were heard outside the train. "They're firing at the engineer!" Matthew said as David and Ryker headed in that direction.

"Hold it!" David and Ryker turned at the voice. It was the Pinkerton agent they saw earlier.

"What is going on?" David said.

The man flashed a badge. "I am Emil Moss, Mister Stewart," the man said. "Pinkerton Agent."

"How do you know my name?" David asked.

"I know the names of everyone on this train," Moss said. "You were all checked out thoroughly before you were allowed to board because we are providing security for a gold shipment this trip."

"The one at Fort Laramie?"

"The same, but I suspect these robbers don't know that. They think the gold is still on board."

"I used to run the Wells Fargo swing station at –"

"Know that too," Moss interrupted. "And Ryker, you served honorably in the Union army for several years. Both of you did. I could use your help now."

"Sure thing," Ryker said. "You're the boss."

"Mister Ryker, stay here and protect the family and the others in this car. If these outlaws try to board, kill them."

"Well I'll –"

"Kill them."

Ryker gulped. "Yes sir." He looked to Ida Mae, the children, and the ten others in the car. "Best get down behind the seats folks. There might be shootin'."

"Mister Stewart, let's work our way to the front," Moss said.

"I'm right with you," David said, moving along behind the detective.

They were two cars back from the tender, which sat directly behind the steam engine, now sitting quietly on the track. In short order, Moss and David made their way to the engine and saw that the engineer had been wounded, but that he could still operate the train.

"Who are they?" Moss said.

"Never saw them before," the engineer replied. "They are young. Act like they don't know what the heck they are about."

"Where are they?" Moss asked, glancing around.

"After they looked around in here, one jumped on and went up top. The other two argued a lot and then they rode back toward the caboose."

"Can the train move?"

"Not sure," the engineer said. "I need to check the rails to see if they damaged them. If they did, I could tip the engine over."

"Can you do that by yourself?"

"Think so," the engineer said, looking at his arm. "The bleeding's stopped."

"While you're doing that, we'll flush these bandits."

"Okay Mister Moss," the engineer said.

"Stewart, we need to work our way back through the train," Moss said. "There are thirteen cars including the caboose, but only one other passenger car. The rest is freight. They could be anywhere along there. I'll take the outside, you take the inside. Okay?"

"Sounds fine," David said. "If I hear shooting, I'll come running."

"Likewise," Moss said, climbing down to the ground as David made his way past the tender and back to the first car.

David was soon back in the passenger car. "Toby, keep a watchful eye." To the other passengers, he said, "Three robbers are somewhere on or around the train folks, so stay low." So saying, he kept moving. He was gone not more than thirty seconds when, coming from the same direction David had, a young man entered the passenger car holding a gun. Ryker was still watching the departing David, now outside walking around the next attached freight car, and by the time he turned back, it was too late.

"Butch?"

"Ryker?" the young man said. "Toby Ryker? From the swing station at Laramie?"

Ryker grinned. "Yeah, it's me." Then he looked stern and pointed his gun at Bobby Parker. "The Pinkerton guy, Emil Moss, says I'm supposed to shoot you. What in tarnation you think you're doing anyway, you knothead?"

Bobby Parker looked around at Ida Mae, Matthew, Laura, and Pauly. "Aw geez," he said, holstering his gun. "What are you guys doing on this train?"

Ida Mae stared at Bobby Parker. "I'll ask you the same question."

"Well, see, Sundance and another buddy and me, we heard that there was some gold on board this train, and um, well, we kind of thought, well, maybe we'd borrow some of it." He grinned at Ida Mae. "At interest of course. Sort of a loan, you might say."

"Bobby, you aren't fooling us for even one second," Ida Mae said. "You stopped this train to rob it! Shame on you!"

"Ma'am, if I'd known you good folks were on this train, we never would have tried to rob – ah, stop it," Bobby Parker said, blushing.

"Well, just you go on home now," Ida Mae said, "before somebody gets hurt. Or better yet, turn yourself in to that Pinkerton man, Mister Moss."

"He'll blow a hole in me big enough to drive this train through," Bobby Parker said. "I can't do that, ma'am."

Gunfire accompanied by screams and shouts was heard from the rear of the train. A moment later, a man even younger than Bobby Parker came running into the passenger car from the rear. "Let's high-tail it out of here, Butch!" he yelled.

"Butch?" A hidden voice from one of the passengers said. "Butch Cassidy?"

"Coming, Sundance," Bobby Parker said. "He tipped his hat to Ida Mae as he followed his partner to the front of the train. "I'm so sorry about this, Missus Stewart. Honest, I am." He smiled at Laura. "It's Laura, isn't it?" Then he bumped into the Sundance Kid.

"Let's rob a train!" Sundance said mockingly. "Gold just sitting there! It'll be so easy! Geez, what a dunce!"

"Well, there is!" Bobby protested. "Somewhere."

"That gold exited several miles back at Fort Laramie, boys," Ryker said. "Right train, wrong spot. Course, I suppose you could attack the fort and rob it, but that might be a bit dangerous."

Sundance saw Ryker's revolver. "You aren't going to shoot us, are you?"

"Mister Pinkerton Man says I'm supposed to but no, I ain't a-goin'to," Ryker said. "I suggest you two find another line of work. Being robbers doesn't suit you very well."

"You think you know it all don't you, grandpaw," Sundance said.

"I know that if you keep this up, you'll die bloody, boys," Ryker replied softly.

"Maybe, but this sure beats getting old and having to eat nothing but greens and oatmeal every day," Bobby said.

Ryker smiled a tired smile at Bobby. "There's some truth to that, Butch." At the sound of boot steps on the car behind them he added, "Now the both of you, get the heck out of here." So saying, he dropped his gun on the floor.

"We're sorry about all of this folks," Bobby said. "You can come out of hiding, because unless the last batch of passengers all took off their boots and forgot them on the train, I see several of you scrunched behind those seats. We never meant to hurt you."

David Stewart and Emil Moss entered the passenger car from the rear moments after Bobby Parker and the Sundance Kid disappeared out the front.

"They were slick, Mister Moss," Ryker said, picking up his gun. "They got the drop on me and then they got clean away. There were two of them but they never got nothin' though, except a tongue-lashin' from me." He looked around at Ida Mae and the others, silently daring them to challenge him, but no one said different.

"Killed one out back," Emil Moss said. "We laid him out on the flat car. The other two just rode off, but I think Mister Stewart winged one of them." David, standing behind Moss, shook his head to the contrary.

"This is all so senseless," Ryker said. "They said they were after the gold. It ain't even on the train no more, and one man is dead for nothin'."

Moss just grunted then walked to the front of the passenger car and out toward the engine. "Is anyone hurt here?" David asked.

"We're fine," Toby said.

"Let's check on the engineer," David said. "He's been wounded."

The outlaws had indeed attempted to derail the train by pulling a piece of track. It took the engineer and two of the crew a half hour to get the track again set properly. In less than an hour from the time the drama began, the train was back in motion. By pushing it, they were able to make up for lost time to the point that by the next morning, they were back on schedule.

Laura was strangely quiet the next day. About mid-afternoon, Ida Mae noticed her staring out the window with tears in her eyes. She leaned over and clasped her daughter's hands. "Laura, what is troubling you?"

Sobbing, Laura looked up at her. "Yesterday Grandpa Ryker said that Bobby will die bloody, Mama," she said. "I don't want that to happen to him."

"I don't either honey," Ida Mae said. "But that is a decision Bobby Parker must make for himself. He is a man now and stands at a fork in the road. Let us pray that he chooses the right path." Ida Mae figured Bobby had already made that decision and crossed the line, but didn't feel like telling Laura that. Although just eleven, Laura was already developing the heart of a woman and she didn't want to be the one to crush it.

The experience of the previous day also had a moving effect upon Pauly. Rather than tease Laura about her concern for Bobby Parker, he sat by her now, looked up at her seriously, patted her arm, and then rested his head against her shoulder.

Deadwood Days

CHAPTER FIVE

The Stewarts arrived in the bustling gold camp of Deadwood without further incident. After renting space at the livery and storing their livestock and likewise their goods at a warehouse, they checked into a small hotel on Main Street. It was 90

noisy and not where they wanted to spend a considerable amount of time, but at least it got them out of the weather. The very next day David and Ida Mae went house hunting and found a vacant house with a barn on the edge of town. They decided to rent it for temporary use and by the end of the week they were moved in. They also purchased a lot near Mount Moriah cemetery and contracted with a stonemason to begin work on their own home, a large, foursquare design with an attic and a carriage house behind. David, accomplished carpenter that he was, intended to do most of the interior woodwork himself.

"Light me up, Ryker."
"Sure thing, Alice." Ryker struck a match against his heel and held it to the end of Poker Alice's cigar.

"Ya sure know how to treat a lady, you old hog," Alice said, picking something bloody out of her nose, wiping it on her pants leg, and belching.

"I don't know about a lady, but I know how to treat you Alice," Ryker said. "Let's play us another game of five card stud."

"Don't think so," Poker Alice said. "Already took you for ten bucks on stud poker." She nudged him. "Maybe we should go upstairs and check out that potato in your britches."

"The one in the front or the one in the back," Ryker asked.

"Ryker, you're a piece of work," Alice said, laughing. "I never thought you'd show your face back here after shooting old Willy Krump in the butt the way you did."

"Didn't shoot him in the hinder exactly," Ryker said. "More in the leg. But he sure carried on. And that's why I'm back here. They went and charged me with murder, Alice."

"Heard about that. They dropped them charges though."

"Not before John McQuiston come a-huntin' me. We killed him outside of Laramie."

"Good riddance," Poker Alice said. "That bounty hunter was crazy." She paused. "Come to think of it, guess I haven't seen him strutting around here lately."

"Yeah, we killed him and you folks dropped the murder charge, but you're still saying I assaulted old Billy Bump or whatever the heck his name was."

"Krump."

"Huh?"

"Krump. Willy Krump was his name. Well, talk to Bullock about it."

"I intend to. Tomorrow, in fact. Don't cotton to having a charge again' me. I might be many things, but I ain't no criminal." He looked at her seriously. "I don't really care about Willy Krump because he was in on the massacre of my wife and daughter years ago. He's burning in hellfire where he belongs. I do care about his family though. I don't want to see them go without."

"You worry about that way more than I would," Alice said, using the spittoon at her feet.

"Maybe," Ryker said, "but I do." He glanced around. "How long you been dealing poker here in this joint anyway?"

44

"Eleven years, maybe twelve. Can't remember, Toby."

"Time flies when you're having fun, doesn't it Alice?"

"Yup. It goes even faster when you're half drunk most of the time," she cackled, revealing a toothless mouth. "You ever tried any of that opium them Chinese got down in the dens?"

"Naw, whiskey was always my poison. Nowadays I just sip a glass of wine now and then."

"Wine? Suppose you drink tea out of a cup too," Alice said, mimicking a high society lady sipping tea out of an imaginary cup with her pinky finger raised.

"I do what I got to do to stay alive, Alice," Ryker said. "That's what Ida Mae Stewart taught me after I had my heart attacks."

Alice looked at Ryker seriously. "Heart attacks? Ryker, you had heart attacks?"

"Yup."

"Well, you're plumb lucky to be here at all then."

"That I am," Ryker agreed. "But I'm here to clear my name and to turn the Potato Creek mine over to David Stewart, that's Ida Mae's husband. He's an old friend of mine. We served in the cavalry together back in the old days, and way back in sixty-two when he was just a young squirt, I saved him from being killed in the Sioux Uprising in Minnesota. He and her and their kids moved up here with me all the way from Laramie."

"The Potato Creek Mine, huh? You seen Johnny yet?"

"No, ain't been out to see Tater Creek Johnny yet but I'll get there." Ryker arose. "It's been good to see you Alice, you old heifer. I'll look in on you again, but right now have to head home for supper."

"You really are concerned about Willy Krump's woman and kid, ain't you?"

"Yeah I am. It ain't their fault he was a worthless coyote."

"Well, I'll be damned."

"Alice, we probably both will be."

Poker Alice threw back her head and laughed. "Ryker, you're all right. Here." She tossed him a ten dollar gold piece. "Take your ten bucks back. Give it to the Krumps."

Ryker took the coin, flipped it into the air, caught it, and pocketed it. "You're all right too, Alice." Then he noticed a tall, well-dressed couple enter the saloon. "Wow, now there's a pair of dandies."

"Yeah, that's Doctor Richard Strachan and his wife Kathy."

"Doctor Strachan?" Ryker said. "He a dentist? I don't like dentists."

"Nah, he's one of them teaching doctors, them fancy professors from back east," Poker Alice said. "One of them whatchamacallems, them arch...archeologists. Digs up old bones and such. He and his lovely wife come out here a couple times a year to gamble. He is very good, I can tell you that. Comes in with fifty and walks out with five hundred every darn time."

"He good at dice, too?"

"Dice, cards, roulette, craps, even the one-armed bandits. You name it."

"Does he cheat?"

"No, but he does have a system, I think. I asked him about it once and all he would say was that it was a question of mathematics. Said something about pies are square."

"Pies are square?" Ryker snorted. "Well, he maybe knows his cards but he doesn't know anything about pies. Everybody knows pies are round." He nodded toward Kathy Strachan. "She gamble too?"

"Nope," Poker Alice said, snubbing the ash from her cigar. "She's a singer. Has the prettiest voice you ever did hear. She sings a version of *Greensleeves* that'll melt your heart."

"Wonder what she ever saw in him?"

"Who knows?" Alice replied. "They say love is blind, you know. But you don't want to cross her. She's fast with a gun. Saw her and Calamity Jane get into a cat fight in here back in, when was that, must have been about eighteen and eighty or so, and I thought for sure she was going to shoot Calamity dead."

"Geez, what were they fighting about?"

"Him," Alice said, hooking her thumb at Doc Strachan who stood by the roulette table. He had pulled a small notebook from his pocket and was jotting something into it. He already had accumulated several gold coins before him. "Jane tried to put the move on him and Kathy, she was defending her territory. She sure taught Calamity to mind her own business. To this day Calamity stays clear of Deadwood when she knows the Strachans are in town."

"Tough customer," Ryker said. "Well, got to mosey on home. See ya, Alice."

"Don't make yourself a stranger, Ryker," Poker Alice said, shuffling her deck.

"Won't," came the reply.

"Evening' Ida Mae, David, kids," Ryker said, entering the house.

"Toby," Ida Mae said. "Did you enjoy your walk?"

"Immensely," Ryker said. "The scenery between here and Rapid City is lovely."

Ida Mae cocked her eye at Ryker. "Um-hum."

"The Potato Creek Mine is a fine one," David said. "I checked it all over today and talked to the men." He looked at Ida Mae and Ryker, his eyes gleaming. "You can see the gold in the walls there. You can almost smell it."

"You met Stumpy Geroux then," Ryker said.

"Yes, I did," David said, chuckling. "I thought you were a character, but your partner takes the cake."

"Stumpy's a good old boy," Ryker said. "But he's anxious to get back to Canady where he has kin. He's plumb tired of working, just like me."

"He told me that," David said. "In fact, he plans to pack his belongings and be out of here by the end of the week. I invited him over to supper."

"I'll set another plate then," Ida Mae said. "I hope he likes roast pork and all the trimmings."

Ryker licked his lips. "Stumpy will eat anything so long as it's roast pork and trimmings."

"I'm afraid that's too rich for you Toby, especially the broth. I'll make you a salad."

"Gee thanks, Sarge," Ryker said.

"Well," Ida Mae relented, "maybe you can have a small slice with the fat removed."

"You're all heart."

"Dad, can I go up to the mine with you one of these days?" Matthew said. "It's boring around here."

"Yup, day after tomorrow," David said. "In fact, if you are interested, I would like to offer you a job to learn mining first hand." He squinted at his eldest son. "Some day you will be the president of that mine."

Stumpy Geroux showed up early for supper. He had a hint of whiskey on his breath and walked a bit unsteadily, but was cordial and had obviously taken a bath and even put on clean long handles and denim pants. "Ain't often I get to meet the new boss and his family," Stumpy said.

"It is our pleasure, Mister Geroux," Ida Mae said. "Geroux...that has to be French."

"Yes, I'm a Frenchy all right," Stumpy said. "Was born In Canady, up above Minnesota. It was in Minnesota though where I met up with Toby Ryker there, nigh onto a hundred years ago when he was trappin' for Hudson's Bay."

"Stumpy, now be honest," Ryker said. "It wasn't no hundred years. Seventy-five maybe, but no hundred."

"Since Toby isn't seventy-five, it wasn't that long ago," David laughed. "Stumpy, you don't look a day over sixty."

"Sixty-six to be exact," Stumpy said. "I'm some younger than Toby."

"Ain't everybody?" Ryker said.

"Can you say something in French?" Laura asked.

"Why sure darling," Stumpy said, smiling. *"Combien pour la fillette*? That means, how much for this little girl?"

"Say something to me," Pauly said.

"Okay, um, let's see...*On t'a berce trop pres du mur?* "

"What does that mean?" Pauly asked, looking at his parents.

"That means," Stumpy said, winking at Ida Mae, "As a child, was your cradle rocked to close to the wall?"

The family, even Pauly, laughed at that one.

The supper was up to Ida Mae's usual standards and enjoyed by all. After the supper dishes were cleared, the adults adjourned to the sitting room while Laura and Pauly did the dishes. Matthew escaped such domestic tasks, for he had to feed and bed down the horses for the night. After excusing himself, he headed out to the barn.

"Mister Geroux, how deep do you think those large gold veins run?" David asked.

"They are running true toward the back of our claim and aren't diminishing in height," Stumpy said. "There is a lot of gold there."

"I wish I knew more about mining like the engineers over at the school in Lead do," David said. "I think there may be a more efficient way to remove that gold. We're washing a lot of it right down Potato Creek, I'm sure."

"Tater Creek Johnny doesn't mind that," Stumpy said. "He's taken to panning downstream from us."

"It bears pondering," Ryker said. "You might want to talk to them fellers over at Lead. They know a heap more about that fancy modern mining than Stumpy or I do, although I know that's hard to believe since we're both so dang smart."

"Yes, we're just gold panners," Stumpy said. "If we can't pick it up with our fingers, we figure it's too small to monkey with."

The men and Ida Mae talked mining until well into the evening, and only then did Ida Mae notice that Matthew had not returned from the barn. "Where's Matthew?" she said.

"I don't know," David said. "Didn't he come in?"

"I don't think so, and his chores didn't take that long."

"Well, maybe he went for a walk or something," David said. "It's a nice night."

"He's just a boy," Ida Mae said.

"He's fourteen going on fifteen," David said. "He's a man."

"Even so, I wish he would come home," Ida Mae said. "It will be dark soon."

"Maybe he's found a gal in town," Ryker said, chuckling.

Ryker didn't know how right he was. Even Matthew didn't realize it when he finished his chores and wandered toward the main street of Deadwood looking for something to do. A bored 15-year-old young man on the streets of Deadwood with all its temptations was not a good combination. He found a stick about 4 feet long and picked it up, pushing it ahead of him and doodling with it in the dust. Abruptly, he turned to walk behind the saloons off of the main street.

"Hey there Sandy, come on over here."

Matthew looked up at the sound of the voice. He saw a young man sitting on the back steps to one of the saloons, a bottle of whiskey in his hand. "Name's Matthew Stewart."

"You look like a Sandy to me," the man said, motioning to Matthew's fair hair. "Come over here where I can see you better. I ain't seen you in town before."

"My folks and sister and brother and Grandpa Ryker just moved here," Matthew said, approaching the fellow.

"Just moved here, huh? What did you do that for?"

"My Pa, he took over the Potato Creek Mine."

"He did?" The man sat up. "Your daddy must be David Stewart then."

"Who are you sir?" Matthew asked, remembering well the routine his father had taught him long ago at the swing station outside of Laramie.

"Frankie Malone. I work at the mine with Stumpy and the others." He patted the step next to him. "Plant your butt down here. Let's have us one of what them there Indians calls a powwow."

"Stumpy had supper with us tonight. He talks French. He said my little brother Pauly banged his cradle against the wall once too many times in French." Matthew said, sitting next to Frankie and shaking his head and chuckling.

"Stumpy's a character." Frankie offered his bottle to Matthew. "You a drinking man?"

Matthew smelled the whiskey. "Geez, it smells like kerosene."

"Tastes like it too. Burns all the way down to your toes. But then it makes you feel so-o good." Frankie nudged Matthew with the bottle. "Here, try a swallow or two."

"Never drank anything other than some table wine at Christmas."

"Oh, this is lots better."

"Okay, how do I do it?"

"Well, I just tip it up, fill up my mouth with it and then swallow it all at once," Frankie said.

"Okay, here goes." Matthew tipped the bottle upright, filled his mouth with the burning liquid, and passed the bottle back to Frankie. He plugged his nose and swallowed. For a second or two nothing happened. Then his eyes widened and he started to cough. "Aw-w," he moaned, "I think that *was* kerosene. My guts are on fire!"

"It will go away," Frankie said. "Give it a few minutes. Then you'll feel really good."

"I hope I feel better than I feel now!" Matthew said. "How can you drink that crap anyway?"

"I'm a miner," Frankie said. "We miners drink darn near anything to wash the dust out of our gullets."

"That's why you do it, huh?"

"Yeah, that and cuz we like to get drunk."

The burning in Matthew's gut was beginning to subside and he was surprised to discover that what Frankie said was true. He started to feel very pleasant and warm all over. "Say, this stuff isn't so bad after all. What do you call it?"

"Whiskey."

"No, I mean what kind?"

"Oh heck, I don't know, the wet kind." Frankie squinted at the bottle. "This here is *Old Heaven Hill,* whatever that is."

"Um, Frankie, can I have another taste of that?"

An hour later, Frankie and Matthew had finished off the bottle of *Old Heaven Hill* and solved most of the problems of the world, some of them more than once. Matthew tried to stand up but got so dizzy that he fell backward again. "Shumpin's wrong wid my legs Frankie," he slurred. "They wanna shtay here." He hiccupped and giggled.

"Oh shit," Frankie said. "Maybe you should lie down for a while. I'll come back later and help you get home."

"Might be a good idea," Matthew said. The dizziness was getting worse and he felt flushed. "This shtep feels nice and cool."

How long he lay there he knew not, but when he opened his eyes, he saw an angel sitting next to him. She was about his age, dressed in a white dress, and she was staring at him. She was the most beautiful creature he had ever seen. She offered him a canteen of water from which he took a sip.

"Are you going to be okay?" the angel said.

"Th-think so," he stammered. "I guess I drank too much. I'm not used to it."

"That's too bad," the angel said. "I hope you never do get used to it. My name's Becky Brown. I'm in town shopping with my folks and saw you lying here. I got worried about you."

"I'm Matthew Stewart," Matthew replied. "But I'm ashamed to have you see me like this."

"You are the family that moved to town last week," Becky said.

"My mom is a teacher. She teaches us school at home," Matthew said. It was all he could think to say.

Becky heard a commotion from the bar and knew someone was coming out. "I have to go, Matthew Stewart." She bent over and surprised him by kissing him. "Bye."

Matthew blinked and it seemed to him that as quickly as she had appeared, the angel was gone.

"Hey Matthew Stewart, let's walk you on home." Matthew recognized Frankie's voice. He struggled to his feet and the two of them headed down the alley toward the Stewart house. Matthew's head was beginning to clear but he had a throbbing headache. Fortunately he had his bearings and was able to direct Frankie to the rear door of their house and maneuver there with only minimal assistance from Frankie.

"Thanks Frankie, for walking me home. You want to come in?"

"Um, no, I think I'll just let you face the music on this one by yourself, pal," Frankie said. "*Adios* and good luck." He turned and headed back toward the saloons on the main street.

Matthew sat on the back porch a while and as he did, the image of Becky Brown came back to him. Was she real or was she a dream? He couldn't be sure. Before he had time to dwell on it, the door opened.

"Well, it's about time," Ida Mae said. "She bent down and looked at her son. "Matthew!" She smelled his breath. "You are crocked!"

The combination of everything hit him, especially his mother's chastisement, and Matthew became nauseated. "I'm going to be sick, mom," he whined.

"I should hope so!" Ida Mae huffed. "David!" she yelled through the screen door into the house, "Come out here!"

David, puffing on his pipe and followed by Ryker, appeared at the back door. "What's going on?"

"Your son is stinking drunk, that's what's going on! I'm glad Mister Geroux already departed so he didn't have to witness such a spectacle."

"Young men need to kick up their heels now and again," Ryker said.

"Stay out of this!" Ida Mae snapped.

"Yes, Sarge."

David lit a kerosene lamp as it was now quite dark, and stepped out into the yard. "Matthew, is this true?"

Matthew vomited again. "Yeah dad, it's true," he said, gasping.

"How much did you have to drink?"

"Not that much, I don't think. Met up with a guy named Frankie from the mine. He gave it to me but he drank most of it, I think."

"Frank Malone," David said, nodding his head. "A strapping young fellow and a good, hard worker. "Tell me son, has this experience taught you anything?"

"Never to drink," Matthew said.

"Wrong," David said. "A man can drink now and again. But a man has to know his limit." He shook Matthew's shoulders. "I think you just learned yours. Just wait until the dry heaves hit you. They are the worst." He took Ida Mae's hand and led her up the steps to the house as Ryker followed behind. "Leave him be. He'll be all right."

"Men!" Ida Mae huffed. "You're all alike!"

"Now Sarge –"

"Hush up!"

Ryker saluted her. "Yes, Sergeant Stewart sir!"

Deadwood Days

CHAPTER SIX

David headed back to the Potato Creek Mine right after breakfast, and Ida Mae taught her children the history of the Deadwood-Lead area based on information she had picked up from the local newspaper office and the few books available on the subject. Matthew had wanted to stay in bed this morning as he was quite hung over from last night's escapade, but Ida Mae showed him no mercy. If anything, she had him up even earlier, telling him to get the barn chores completed and to chop a load of wood before breakfast then take a bath after breakfast so he would be alert during class. He sat and listened to her now, his chin propped on his hand, his eyes blinking much slower than usual.

"Matthew, who was Jack McCall?"

"I do not recall Jack McCall," Matthew said as Laura and Pauly laughed.

"He was an assassin right here in Deadwood who killed Wild Bill Hickok while the pistoleer was engaged in a poker game," Ida Mae said. "It was an unsavory situation all around, but it did indeed happen here. As such, it is a part of local history."

"How did this man kill Wild Bill Hickok?" Pauly asked

"He shot him in the back of the head with a revolver," Ida Mae said.

"Did he die bloody, Mama?" Laura asked, thinking about Bobby Parker.

"To be sure," Ida Mae said. "Although a wound such as that would cause such massive trauma that he probably felt very little if any pain. Wild Bill Hickok died almost instantly."

"What happened to him after he was killed?" Pauly said, leaning forward, keenly interested. Even Matthew and Laura were lured by the gory details.

"As I piece it together, Ellis T. Peirce, a local barber and undertaker who now resides in Rapid City, laid out the corpse until it was interred. Mister Peirce said that even in death, Wild Bill Hickok was the prettiest corpse he had ever seen. Of course, I understand that Mister Peirce is as full of hot air as our own Grandpa Toby Ryker is."

"Interred?" Pauly wrinkled up his nose.

"Buried, Pauly, buried. Wild Bill Hickok is buried at Mount Moriah Cemetery up on the hill. We can go up there some time and see his grave if you'd like."

"We'd like that," Laura said.

"Maybe we can have a picnic there," Matthew said.

"Sounds like fun," Pauly said. As his face lit up he added, "Hey! We can play hide-and-go-seek behind the gravestones.

"And there is also the history of the Chinese laborers here, and Calamity Jane..." Ida Mae moved into the next topics with a flawless transition that attested to her professional training.

"Good morning Seth. It's been a while," Ryker said upon entering the Bullock and Star store on main street.

"Why for Pete's sake, if it isn't Toby Ryker! Let me get a look at you." Seth Bullock stepped from behind the counter of the hardware store that he and his partner Sol Star operated in Deadwood. Besides running the store, he was a deputy United States Marshal. "You've trimmed down some."

"Yup, I can look down and see my boots now instead of my belly button," Ryker, said.

"I ain't seen you in nigh onto two years."

"Yeah, it's been about that long since I passed through. That's what I came to see you about, Seth." Ryker pulled the wanted poster out of his pocket and handed it to the lawman.

Seth Bullock opened the poster and studied it a second then leveled his steely grey eyes on Ryker. "This is ancient history. A coroner's inquest ruled that William Krump died of natural causes." He handed the poster back. "You can toss this or throw darts at it or use it for out-house wipe. I heard you folks down Laramie way shot McQuiston for us."

"That we did, deader than a doornail. He have any kin around here?"

"Nope, he was a lone wolf. Hung around the gambling halls and the whores when he wasn't trailing somebody."

"Well then, Sheriff O'Brian most likely already planted him on boot hill in Laramie, I reckon."

"Good. He gave us man-killers a bad name," Seth said jokingly. "So, with the charge against you dropped and McQuiston dead, what's your complaint?"

"You still have an assault charge again' me on your books, which makes me a criminal, Seth. Don't think I'm a criminal, because this here Krump feller was one of them that was in on the killing of my wife and daughter back in the Indian nations."

Bullock stared at Ryker incredulously. "You mean to tell me that Krump was part of that pack of buffalo hunters in that Pawnee camp raid?"

"Um-hum."

The U.S. Marshal shook his head rapidly. "This is all going too fast for me. Sol?" He turned to his partner who was working on the books. "I need to do some law work with Ryker here in the back office. Can you cover the counter?"

An hour later, Ryker had told his tale of how he recognized Willy Krump as one of the murderers of his wife and daughter in that Pawnee camp so many long years ago. He admitted to shooting the man to avenge the death of his family, which Marshal Bullock readily agreed was justifiable under the code of the west. Besides, Bullock said, since Wild Flower and Hope were Indian and the crime was committed on Indian land, the White Man's Law would have limited jurisdiction there anyway. Ryker had no choice but to call the man out for retribution.

Ryker told him the only part of the demise of Willy Krump that disturbed him was that he contributed to taking away the support from Krump's widow and daughter, whom he heard were now nearly desti-tute. Bullock confirmed that this was true and suggested an attorney, the Honorable Hiram Thaddeus Custis, for Ryker could tell his story to.

"Suppose I should arrest you and lock you up, there being a warrant out over that assault charge," Seth said, maintaining a straight face.

"You'll never take me alive." Ryker snapped his fingers. "Hey, I got a peachy idea. I'll go home and strap on my gun belt then at high noon, you can call me out on Main Street right out front here. That ought to drum up some business for the store."

"You'd probably get lucky and shoot me," Bullock replied.

"Ain't that fast anymore," Ryker replied, grinning. "More likely I'd shoot myself in the foot while I was tryin' to draw."

"I know," the marshal conceded, laughing. Then I'd have your doctor bill to pay for. "Besides, it's the city sheriff's worry, not mine, and he doesn't even know you're in town yet. I'll pull rank on him since he and I don't see eye to eye anyway, and he's local and I'm federal. Let's just say you are released on your personal recognizance until this is cleared up. That's how I'll enter it in the books. By the way, you hear about the hangings?"

"Why no, I ain't."

"We brought in three renegade Sioux from the Rez who scalped, butchered, and robbed two white families east of the hills out on the plains. Caught the devils red-handed so to speak, and they still had some of the stolen goods with them. We suspect they've been raiding for some time and killed others too, but had no proof. This time we do. They've been tried and sentenced to hang."

"When's the necktie party?" Ryker asked.

"This Saturday at high noon on the courthouse square," Seth said. "We're fixing up the gallows. Come on down if you want to see justice done."

"I'll tell the family about it," Ryker said.

"We're also looking for a hangman. Pays five dollars a head."

Ryker gulped. "Well Seth, like you know, I done lots of things in my time including hanging scoundrels, but that was a long time ago and I ain't got the stomach for it anymore. Think I'll pass."

"Guess I'll have to do it myself then, like always," Seth said. "I don't mind hanging butchers like these though, and Indians, they're usually pretty quiet about it. They don't whine and carry on like whites do."

"You got them over to the jail?"

"Yup, all ready to have their necks stretched."

"Do ya mind if I jaw with them a mite?"

"Suppose it would be okay, you being an old cavalry scout and all," Seth said. "I can trust you not to slip them a weapon or a file or anything like that, can't I?"

"Seth! What kind of a conniving yahoo do you think I am?"

"Sure, come on over," Seth said, laughing. "Two of them don't say much, but Big Nose Charlie, he likes to talk. He's actually quite entertaining. Kind of hate to string him up."

Ryker and Marshal Bullock entered the jail, the marshal removing the key ring from the hook on the wall and opening the cell door that led to the small cellblock to the rear of the building. There were three single cells and a bullpen with six bunks off of it. It was in the bullpen that the three condemned men awaited their fate. They lay on the cots and turned as the two men entered, but only one of them arose. The other two rolled over and faced the wall.

"This is Big Nose Charlie," Marshal Bullock said. He motioned to the other two. "That is Dakota Spears and that one over there is Ron Tuttle."

Ryker pulled up a chair, sat on it backward, and rested his arms on the pressed back. "Howdy, Charlie, my name's Toby Ryker."

Charlie sat on his bunk next to Ryker. "Hey Seth, how about giving me some cigarette fixings?"

"Okay Charlie," Seth said, tossing a sack of tobacco to Charlie. "Don't set your mattress on fire and burn up."

Charlie made up a smoke and Seth lit him up. "And cheat you out of your hanging fee? I wouldn't do that, Seth. You know me better than that."

"I'll leave you two be," Seth said. "Toby, when you are ready to leave just say so. I'll be out front."

"Okay Seth, thanks."

Raising his hand at Ryker, Charlie said, "How, white man."

"I suppose if I was in your moccasins, I would be bitter too."

Charlie studied Ryker a minute then sighed. "Oh, it isn't that," he said. "I knew it would come to this. I'm ready to be hung. They can have my body but..." he placed his hand over his heart, "they can't have my spirit."

"You know, I lived among the Indians quite a spell," Ryker said. "The Pawnee down in the southwest, and among the Crow, and even among the Ojibwe and the Dakota up in Minnesota. I was married for a spell to a Pawnee Princess. She was the daughter of the shaman, Far Sight Man."

"I heard of him," Big Nose Charlie said. "Most every tribe has. They were slaughtered by you whites."

"Whites can be devils too," Ryker said. They were buffalo hunters and they killed not only Far Sight Man, but my wife Wild Flower and my daughter Hope. She was but five when they came into the village and did it. We took our revenge on them and killed them in return."

"You killed your own kind?" Big Nose Charlie said, surprised.

"Yes, I did. I was more Pawnee than white at that time and in fact, I'm half Ojibwe by blood. Anyway, one of those devils got away, but I remembered him. Shot him less than two years ago right here in Deadwood after I rejoined the whites."

"Well now, if that don't beat all," Charlie said.

"Now you know why I killed white folks, but why'd you kill white folks, Charlie?"

"Because we are warriors! We have been for many ages even before you whites came to this land. That's what we do. Back in the old days, we would have taken them captive and made slaves out of the women and children, but I don't know, we all got drunked up and things got out of hand."

"There are reservations nowadays, Charlie, like you know, so it ain't necessary to rob and kill anymore to survive. The government will help you."

"Reservations!" Big Nose Charlie spat out the word. "Have you ever been to Pine Ridge? Barren wastelands you mean. Your government starves us, takes away our pride, and tells us we can't practice our Sun Dance. Your government says we shouldn't fish and hunt buffalo to live, teaches our children your language and your way of life, dresses us in your clothes, gives us disease, makes us drunk and weak in the mind…your government has just found another way of conquering us like we conquered others. Only there is no honor to it."

"So is there honor to slaughtering families of whites out on the plains who are trying to survive and who had nothing to do with putting you on a reservation?" Ryker asked.

Big Nose Charlie smiled. "You are a philosopher, Mister Toby Ryker. I must be honest and admit that I never quite worked that one through in my own head either. It's just that those whites and the others we killed became a symbol of our rage." He paused. "Kind of like Custer."

"Custer was a jackass," Ryker said. "But those two families, do you now regret killing them?"

"Yes. If they'd died with dignity or made a good fight of it like a warrior, it would have been better. But most of them didn't. The way they screamed and cried was like skinning a pup for the stew pot. There was no honor in that."

Ryker shook his head. "Well, I did some things in my time that I'm not proud of either. That one I shot here in Deadwood, it didn't really accomplish anything. My family is still gone, and now his family is wanting."

The two men were silent for several minutes, each lost in his private thoughts. Big Nose Charlie spoke next. "Anyway, it doesn't matter," he said, hooking his thumbs together and flapping his hands like wings. "Soon, my spirit will soar with the eagle to a better place."

"I hope that's what happens to mine when I die," Ryker said, also hooking his thumbs and flapping his hands like wings.

Big Nose Charlie looked at Ryker. "That time is not too far off for you."

"How do you know that, Charlie."

"I can see it in your eyes, which shows me your spirit. It won't happen right away, but you are tired."

"You are wise, Charlie. In earlier times you could have been a great leader."

"In an earlier time, I never would have lived to adulthood," Big Nose Charlie said. "That is the irony of all of this. I was born with a disease that would have killed me many years ago except for the white man's medicine. In fact, a few years ago I was in jail and real sick and waiting to be hung just like now, and your medicine cured me again. I escaped from there."

"Well, we sure wouldn't want to hang a sick Indian," Ryker said. "You know, the older I get the more I realize there isn't a lot of sense to what happens, is there?"

"Not hardly," Big Nose Charlie said. "What is destined to happen will happen. Say, are you coming to my hanging? I don't think I'm going to escape from it this time. These bars of Seth's are too tight."

"Do you want me to?"

"Yes," Big Nose Charlie said. "I consider you a kindred spirit and would like to look out onto a face that understands me as I travel to the next world."

"Does dying scare you at all?"

"Nah," Charlie said. "Like I said earlier, I already lived years longer than I had a right to. I enjoyed many wives who bore me strong sons. And as for hanging, it just takes a second. Seth out there, he knows how to place a rope."

"I'll sure be there then. Can't speak for the rest of my family, but I'll be there to see you off." Ryker arose and replaced the chair then clasped hands with Charlie through the jail bars.

"By the way, ask Seth to bring me back a nice big steak on Saturday morning," Charlie said. "I read somewhere that you whites always offer your condemned a steak dinner before you hang them."

"I'll do that," Ryker said.

"Wouldn't want to die hungry. And make sure it's Hereford. No longhorn. I hate longhorn. Too stringy."

"It'll be Hereford if I got to butcher it myself," Ryker said. "Charlie, do you suppose anyone will remember us?"

"If our names were Custer or Hickok maybe," Charlie said. "But Toby Ryker, Big Nose Charlie...nah."

"Maybe somebody will put us in a book." Ryker said. He and Charlie stared at each other a moment then started laughing, Ryker slapping his knee and Charlie snorting.

"Doubt that," Charlie said, wiping his eyes.

"Well now, you never can tell," Ryker said. "Maybe some writer will come along and put us in a book sometime."

"It would have to be a writer with nothing better to do," Charlie said, snorting again. "And he probably wouldn't recognize an Indian if one sat on him." He shook his head. "Probably nobody would read it anyway."

"Don't be so sure. Look at that oddball Edgar Poe. He was crazy as a hoot owl and they read his stories. Stuff about telltale hearts and pendulums and crazy stuff like that."

"Doctor McGillicuddy had Poe in his library when he was Indian Agent at Pine Ridge," Charlie said. "He's the one who's going to make sure we're dead on Saturday."

"See? It could happen." Ryker nodded his head. "Maybe people will remember us." Both chuckled again as he arose to leave.

"I won't hold my breath until that happens." Charlie said. "I do feel bad about being a disappointment to Doctor McGillycuddy though. He's been a great friend to the Lakota. We call him *Wasicu Wakan,* which means Holy White Man."

"We all do things we regret," Ryker said. "At least you are at peace with yourself."

"That I am."

"Adios, Charlie. See you at the hanging."

"I'll be there, and Seth will make sure I'm on time."

"Seth! I'm ready!" Ryker hollered, rattling the cell door.

"Hello, Matthew Stewart."

Matthew looked around from his chores in the barn and saw Becky Brown standing in the doorway. "Becky! It's wonderful to see you again. Come on inside."

"You look like you feel better than you did the last time I saw you."

Matthew blushed. "Yeah well, I feel better. I'm so sorry you saw me like that. You know, when I really came to, I wasn't sure if you were real or if you were the most wonderful dream I'd ever had in my life."

"I'm real all right," Becky said. "I told my Mama that you said your mama was teaching school at your house. Do you suppose I could come there some days and learn some ciphering and stuff?" She looked down. "It's embarrassing to not know numbers and writing and all."

"Becky, I'm sure my mom would love to have you as a student," Matthew said. "Let's go inside and I will introduce you to her."

"My Pa doesn't make much money so we can't pay her." Becky moved over to Matthew, took the pitchfork from him and threw it away. "Maybe there is some other way I can pay for it." She kissed him on the lips.

"Matthew, come here! Is someone in the barn with you?" Ida Mae hollered.

"Coming Ma," Matthew said. "Geez, I swear she has eyes in the back of her head."

"I think all mothers do," Becky said, laughing.

"Yeah, well I wish she would close them once in a while," Matthew said. "Come on, I'll introduce you to her." Hand in hand, Matthew and Becky left the barn and headed toward the house.

"Well now, I thought I saw two people in there," Ida Mae said. "Matthew, who is this lovely young lady?"

"This is Becky mom, Becky Brown. We just met the other night."

"I'm very pleased to meet you Becky," Ida Mae said. "Is that a nickname for Rebecca?"

"Why, yes ma'am, it is," Becky said. "But nobody calls me Rebecca. Everybody just calls me Becky. Matthew told me you teach school. That's why I came over today."

"Would you like to come to my school?" Ida Mae asked. "Right now it is just my children, but when our new house is built, we will have a classroom there."

"I would love to, Missus Stewart," Becky said. "It's powerful sad not being able to cipher and such."

"Ladies should know of such things and of the arts," Ida Mae said. "I can offer you the basics of reading, writing, and arithmetic. If you want more than that you need to go to the normal school in Rapid City."

"I'll gladly settle for the basics," Becky said. "That's more than I have now. I don't know how I will pay you though. My folks don't make much money and they have four boys besides me to tend to."

"We'll work something out," Ida Mae said. "Don't fret about that. I'm delighted you want to learn. For now, that's payment enough for me, and I have several books you can borrow."

"Thank you, Mrs. Stewart. I really appreciate this." "You are most welcome," Ida Mae said. "Where do you live?"

"Out of town a ways toward the mines."

"That is a long walk. Matthew, hitch up the team. I need to run a few errands in town anyway. We will give Becky a ride home and meet her family."

"Yes mom. Come on Becky, I'll show you how to harness a horse."

That evening as the rest of the family sat around the dinner table dining on pork chops, potatoes and beans, Ryker put his oatmeal to his lips. "You folks like to take in a hanging come Saturday?" he said pleasantly. "They drop the trap at noon. We can have lunch after."

Ida Mae, who had just taken a mouthful of potatoes and gravy, began to choke on it. David rushed to her side and patted her on the back as Ryker and the children looked on.

"Ida Mae, are you all right?" David said.

"Water," she croaked, her eyes tearing up." He handed her a glass of water, which she sipped gratefully. "Yes, I'm all right now." She took a deep breath. "Toby! What a thing to say at the table!"

"Oh, you mean about putting the noose to the necks of those heathens?"

"Yes. Please let's discuss this after supper in the parlor, if it can wait until then," Ida Mae said.

"Yeah, sure Sarge," Ryker said, looking from her to David and the kids, bewildered. "It can wait. They ain't goin' nowhere, locked up in the jailhouse like they are."

After the supper dishes were cleared, the family joined Ryker in the parlor. "See," he began, "Marshal Bullock let me talk to them fellers over in the jailhouse. Lakota Indians, they are, but most folks call them Sioux. Killed two families of white settlers out on the plains and have been sentenced to hang. There are three of them. The hanging is Saturday morning on the courthouse square. Seth said we could come if we have a mind to and witness justice done. There will be a crowd."

There was silence in the room as Ryker looked pleasantly at the three young faces staring back at him then at Ida Mae, who had gone white, and at David, who shifted uncomfortably, took out his pipe, and lit it.

Matthew spoke first. "They are actually going to kill them right there then?"

"Um-hmm," Ryker said. "Snap their necks. They kick a little bit until they choke. It doesn't take but a few seconds."

"Have you ever seen anyone get hung before, Grandpa?" Pauly asked.

"Yeah, a few times. In fact, I was in on the execution of thirty-eight Sioux warriors all at one time up in Mankato Minnesota back in sixty-two. It happened after the Great Sioux Uprising." Ryker looked down and shook his head. "That was a sad day, December 26, 1862, the day after Christmas. I'll never forget it." He sighed and looked from Pauly to David. "That's about the time I first met up with your pa, but he was just a little tadpole then about your age, Laura. Since then we hung a few ourselves, didn't we, David?"

"Yes we did," David replied. "Murderers and two rapists down near the border. Back in our cavalry days." He looked seriously at the children. "It isn't a pretty sight, kids. I'll warn you of that. But it is how we administer justice to those who commit horrible crimes upon others. As such, it is a good lesson to see and it is something you will never forget. That hanging in Minnesota that Toby spoke of, I did not get to see." He sighed, paused, and looked out the window. "But those Indians killed my three older brothers and my parents and took me as a hostage, and that I had to watch. It was just lucky for me that Toby came along or else they would have killed me too."

Everyone in the room was silent as David wiped tears from his eyes. Ryker finally broke the silence. "An execution is a darn sight more dignified a death than the massacre the Sioux inflicted upon them poor white settlers back in Minnesota in sixty-two, and that these three out here did to those two families, you can bet your bottom dollar on that. These heathens showed them no mercy at all. Had times been different, it could have been us out there on them plains that got butchered."

"I don't approve of the government executing anyone," Ida Mae said. "Why don't they put them in prison and force them to work hard for the rest of their lives and do penance for the common good?"

"Some do," David said, "but murderers, cutthroats, and crazies like I heard tell these three are, well, they are beyond redemption. It is best they are put to death lest they break free and commit more murders."

"I catch your drift," Ida Mae replied, "but let us just say that I don't agree the government has the right to execute one of its citizens no matter how vile. That makes the government no better than the creature it is killing." She looked at the children. "I shall leave it up to you. If you wish to attend this execution with your father and Grandpa Ryker, so be it. I shall not go."

"Think I'll watch it," Matthew said.

"Matthew, you can write it up as a theme for class," Ida Mae said.

"I'll go too," said Pauly. "I'll hide behind Papa if it gets too scary."

"I'm not," Laura said. "Maybe it is justified but I think it is barbaric. There are some things in this world that I don't need to see, like those ugly alligators in Florida, even if they are real." She ran to her mother and hugged her.

"It's settled then," Ryker said. "Us men folk will go to the hanging, and Ida Mae, Laura, I do appreciate your thoughts on this, believe me I do. Like I told Big Nose Charlie, that's one of the Sioux that's getting' hung, there's a lot of things that get done that don't make sense. Like killing Pawnee Princesses and innocent settlers, putting Indians on reservations and making them prisoners in their own land, maybe even hanging criminals by their necks until they choke, but these are our times and I guess maybe we don't know any better." He approached Ida Mae and Laura and laid his big hands on their shoulders, embracing them. "I hope that in future years, people get more civilized so none of this is necessary. And wise men and women like you two are the ones who will make that happen."

Deadwood Days

CHAPTER SEVEN

Saturday morning rolled around quickly. The men were up as usual and after a late breakfast dawdled around the house, the execution obviously on their minds. Ryker left about 9:30, returning an hour later. When the mantle clock in the parlor struck a single chime signaling the half hour at 11:30, David stood and stretched. He and Pauly and Matthew with tablet and pencil in hand, along with Ryker, departed for the courthouse lawn.

A crowd had already begun to trickle in, dampened somewhat no doubt by the overcast skies that threatened to rain on the festivities. Several carried parasols in the event that such an act of God were to occur. Ryker, David, and the boys got a front row view close to the gallows and stood there milling around and waiting. Ryker saw Ellis "Doc" Peirce, whom it seemed everyone in the Hills knew, dressed in flamboyant black garb and driving a horse-drawn wagon containing three wooden coffins, rein his team to a halt on the other side of the gallows. He jumped down from the seat, grabbed a guitar from the wagon box, mounted the steps of the gallows and scanned the crowd.

"My oh my," he began, glancing skyward. "What a wonderful day for a hanging." He tipped his black top hat. "Welcome to the Deadwood Hangman's Festival, ladies and gentleman, boys and girls. Step right up to see real live subjects hung before your very eyes. We have three fine specimens of degenerate humanity to send to perdition to-day." He motioned toward the jailhouse with a wave of his hand.

As though on cue, the door opened and Seth Bullock came out carrying a shotgun followed by Big Nose Charlie, Ron Tuttle, and Dakota Spears who were in chains. Behind them were two deputies also with shotguns and Doctor Valentine McGillicuddy, a physician from Rapid City. As they walked toward the gallows, Doc Peirce strummed his guitar and began to sing, to the tune of *The Streets of Larado:*

> As I walked out in the streets of old Deadwood
> As I walked out in old Deadwood one day
> I spied a dead Indian all wrapped in white linen
> All wrapped in white linen and cold as the clay

The crowd began to hoot and cheer and Ryker saw Doc tip his top hat again. He glanced around and saw Poker Alice puffing on her usual cigar, and next to her, a famous face. Nudging David, he pointed her out. "There's Calamity Jane over there!" He waved at her and she put two fingers to her mouth and whistled sharply.

"Hi, Ryker!" Calamity Jane hollered.

"Seriously folks," Doc Pierce continued, "the ladies from the First Baptist Church are here with us today, and along with the Reverend Thomas Charmichal, they wish to lead us in prayer." He motioned to a man and several ladies in the crowd. "Come right on up to the front here, folks."

Reverend Charmichal and five women moved to the base of the gallows and turned to face the crowd. "My brothers and sisters," Reverend Charmichal began, "we gather together today on this solemn occasion to witness three red heathen savages go unto their Maker and atone for their sins." While the minister spoke, Ryker noticed Marshal Bullock remove his watch, glance at it, and nod to his two deputies. They nudged the three prisoners with the barrels of their shotguns, who started walking toward the gallows. When they got to the steps, the condemned began to ascend, looking up at the single noose that dangled above the trap door.

"These men committed atrocities upon their fellow man with unspeakable cruelty, snuffing the lives from the Jackson family and the Addams Family, both of this Territory. We commend their souls unto the Lord our God for whatever punishment awaits them for all eternity. Please join us now in song and in memory not of these evil, vile monsters, but of those innocents, our neighbors, whom they put to death." Reverend Charmichal blew into a pitch pipe then raised his hands above the ladies of the church, and on the downbeat they began to sing *Shall We Gather at the River*. "Please join us!" he shouted to the crowd as he began to clap his hands to the rhythm of the hymn.

Once the song began, Ryker began to tap his foot and clap his hands to the beat of the music. He glanced down at Pauly and grinned at him, and Pauly clapped his hands too. Knowing some of the words and the refrain, Ryker belted it out off-key but with gusto:

> Shall we gather at the river
> Where bright Angel feet have trod
> With its crystal tide forever
> Flowing by the throne of God
>
> Yes, we'll gather at the river
> The beautiful…the beautiful…river…
> Gather with the saints at the river
> That flows by the throne of God
>
> Soon we'll reach the shining river
> Soon our pilgrimage will cease
> Soon our happy hearts will quiver
> With the melody of peace
>
> Yes, we'll gather at the river
> The beautiful…the beautiful…river…
> Gather with the saints at the river
> That flows by the throne of God.

Although Ryker was not a church-going man, the rousing hymn stimulated him as none ever had before. It was sort of comforting, he thought, to realize that once these earthly cares are cast aside there was a vast universe, another dimension to be explored. Would he be reunited with Wild Flower and Hope? Were they awaiting him on the other side? It occurred to him that most certainly they were. He guessed that during these few moments this was as close to prayer, to a true religious experience, that he had ever come.

"By the power vested in me as United States Marshal of Dakota Territory, I order you, Ronald Tuttle, Dakota Spears, and Big Nose Charlie Lamore, to be hung by the neck until you are dead. May God have mercy on your souls."

The chilling words of Marshal Seth Bullock brought Ryker out of his reverie. He glanced toward the scaffold as Seth removed Ron Tuttle from the chains that secured him from the other two criminals and maneuvered him over the trap door of the gallows. He grabbed the rope noose and quickly placed it over Tuttle's neck, adjusting it to the correct tension and placing the knot next to the cervical vertebrae.

"Do you have any final words?" Bullock said.

Tuttle drew a deep breath and looked soberly out over the crowd then at the marshal and shook his head. Bullock placed a white cloth sack over Tuttle's head then stepped back and grabbed the lever that controlled the trap door. After a brief pause, he pulled the lever. There was an audible gasp from the crowd as the body of Ron Tuttle dropped a couple feet, stopped suddenly in mid-air, kicked once in a reflex motion, and his head slumped forward against the white sack.

Ryker and David glanced at each other, grimly silent. Ryker then wondered what effect this had on the boys. He looked at Matthew, who seemed unperturbed but was busy writing on his tablet. Pauly had taken hold his father's hand and stared now at the sack-covered head of the late Ron Tuttle. With his other hand, he rubbed his neck. None of the Stewarts noticed Dakota Spears watching Pauly.

Doctor Valentine McGillicuddy, after counting three minutes on his watch, moved over to the body of Ron Tuttle. He removed a stethoscope from his bag and placed it over the man's chest even as the body continued to dangle. Satisfied that Tuttle was dead, he nodded to Bullock and Doc Pierce on the gallows. Doc Pierce came down, and he and McGillicuddy with help from David and two other men from the crowd removed the body from the noose and placed it in one of the coffins. The noose was elevated into position again and the trap door reset.

Next, Marshal Bullock positioned Dakota Spears over the trap door the same way as he had Tuttle and placed the noose. "Do you have any last words?" he said.

"Yes," Spears replied, looking straight at Pauly Stewart. "I will come to you in the night when you cannot see me and I will scalp you. I will cut you with my knife and watch you while you suffer and die, little boy!" He laughed demonically and leaned toward Pauly, who screamed in terror as Bullock jerked the Indian back. "I know where your house is." The last thing Pauly saw was that cruel face, those mad eyes, leering down him from above as the sack was drawn over Dakota Spears head. It was an image that was to haunt him relentlessly.

"You vile demon!" Ryker roared, lurching toward the gallows. "What kind of a monster are you anyway? Why don't you try spewing your venom on a man instead of an innocent young boy?"

David held him back. "Toby, don't get worked up about it." He picked up Pauly in his strong arms and hugged his sobbing son. "That man cannot hurt you. I won't let him, Pauly."

The crowd grew unruly at the sight of the killer Indian hurling his last act of defiance. They surged toward the gallows.

"Murderer!" a voice hollered.

"Butcher!" someone screamed.

"Kill them all!" another one said.

"Rotten redskin!" one of the ladies from the Baptist church yelled.

"Even at his hour of doom, a skunk cannot change his stripe," said Doc Peirce.

All the while, Dakota Spears, his face now concealed under the sack, laughed until his shoulders shook.

"Even the devil won't claim him," Ryker huffed. He too caressed Pauly. "It will be all right Pauly. Don't you fret none about that evil monster."

"Step aside, Seth!" Calamity Jane yelled, drawing her pistol. "I'll shoot the red devil right between the eyes for you!"

"Put the gun down, Jane," Seth said, resting his hand on his Peacemaker. "You know better than that." He motioned to a deputy to seize the weapon from Calamity Jane.

"Settle down Calam," Poker Alice said. "As drunk as you are, you're liable to shoot Seth."

Concerned about the actions of the crowd and fearing a riot, Marshal Bullock moved to the trap handle and in the process bumped the rope about Dakota Spears neck, moving the knot from the side to the back. Not noticing it, he sprung the trap.

A few seconds later, the crowd watched Dakota Spears exit this life as angry as he had lived it, no doubt cursing everyone about him including his Creator. But he didn't die easy. The rope did not break his neck as it was supposed to so instead, he strangled to death. He kicked and struggled, which made Pauly cry out louder, fearful that the bully would somehow break free and come after him. When at last his throes subsided and Doctor McGillicuddy pronounced him dead, even the Reverend Carmichal said "Halleluiah!"

Marshal Bullock, red-faced, looked out at the crowd. "I apologize for that, folks. It was a sloppy job." He took a deep breath and turned to the deputies, wiggling his finger. "Bring Charlie."

Ryker watched as the final attraction of the day, the man he met and knew as Big Nose Charlie, stepped forward and was removed from all the chains. He stood on the scaffold totally unbound, smiling pleasantly at the crowd. Looking down at him, he put his thumbs together and flapped his hands like wings. Ryker returned the gesture. Before Marshal Bullock put the noose on Big Nose Charlie, he asked him if he had anything he would like to say.

"Yes, actually, I do," Charlie said. "Do you have a cigarette?" When Bullock obliged him and he lit up, he said, "Fourscore and seven years ago..." and laughed along with the crowd. Even Doc Peirce, who hated to be upstaged, had to laugh. It was a good tension reliever for the crowd, helping them to settle down from the nightmare death of Dakota Spears moments before.

"Good one, Charlie," Peirce hollered. "I'll remember that one."

"First off," Charlie said, "I must apologize for the rude behavior of my companion, Dakota Spears. Even amongst us Indians, it's hard to find good warriors these days. I really thought he would die better than this." He looked down at Pauly. "Your daddy's right, little man. He won't hurt you, and you know something else? I didn't much like him either." He looked back at the crowd. "I understand that I am living in a white man's world now, your world, and I have not lived by your laws. Therefore, I deserve to suffer the consequences of your justice. I don't agree with it but I accept it. Those families we killed, it wasn't supposed to happen that way but it did. For that I am sorry." He looked down at Ryker. "A few days ago I met a philosopher. He was kind enough to bring me a nice Hereford steak this morning so at least I'm being hung on a full stomach." He looked around at the crowd. "Sure beats the hell out of longhorn, doesn't it?" He smiled as the crowd laughed again. "Anyway, it's time to cross the Great Divide, so let's be done with it." He ground out the cigarette. "I'm ready, Seth."

Ryker fixed his eyes on Big Nose Charlie's as Seth placed the noose. Charlie continued to smile even as the sack was put over his head. In a moment, he too was dead. As with the other two bodies, David helped McGillicuddy and Peirce box Big Nose Charlie.

David also made a point of taking Pauly to the coffin of Dakota Spears, opening it, and removing the sack from the now lifeless face of the outlaw. He pointed to the body and told Pauly he could touch it if he wanted to so as to prove to himself that Dakota Spears could not harm him. Pauly did so just once. Since Spears strangled instead of breaking his neck, his airway was blocked, which caused air to become lodged in his lungs. At Pauly's touch the neck moved just enough to release the air from the lungs, resulting in an audible moan from the body.

"His ghost just got out," Pauly said, whimpering and climbing quickly onto his father's lap.

"It will be all right," David said, looking at Ryker and shaking his head. He feared Pauly would be a nervous wreck before this was over.

Doc Peirce headed off with the three coffins. He intended to move them to Custer then prepare them for burial, put up a tent and charge admission to the curious public to come and see the "murderous, cutthroat Indians," all the while telling tall tales about them. When the interest petered out, he would plant the corpses on Boot Hill.

David, now carrying Pauly, Matthew, and Ryker walked home, thinking of the spectacle they had just witnessed. "Well David, they are gone and justice is done," Ryker said.

"Say, were you that philosopher Big Nose Charlie referred to by any chance?"

"As a matter of fact I am. We had a good visit the other day. I took him the steak and ones for the other two also, though I doubt they ate any."

"I have mixed feelings about all this," David said.

"Me too," Ryker agreed. "We were witnessing a clash of races today, that's for darn sure. Tuttle, I don't know about him. He didn't show enough of himself to let us inside. Spears..." he patted Pauly's leg as they walked along, "there are people like him in any race. Mean, evil, hateful men. He was just like McQuiston, the bounty hunter we shot back in the mountains David, only he was an Indian rather than a white man. And then there was Big Nose Charlie." Ryker smiled. "Charlie was born about a hundred years too late. I suspect in an earlier time, he would have been a great leader of his people. But he didn't fit in today's world. He didn't belong here." He hooked his thumbs back of his suspenders. "That happens to a lot of us sooner or later."

"I don't know," David said. "Somehow I just don't feel we were justified in what we accomplished. It is easy to hate Spears because he was so evil, but to take the life of Charlie and Tuttle...I just don't know."

"But if we put them in prison, they'd just get out again, get drunked up and start killing all over again," Ryker said. "I think even Charlie knew it."

"Probably," David agreed. "Maybe Ida Mae's ideas are starting to wear off on me, but then I think of those settlers, helpless and shown no mercy, and I think the other way. It's confusing, Toby."

"Yes it is," Ryker agreed.

David rubbed Pauly's back. "I know one mistake we made today."

"Believe you are right about that David," Ryker said. "If we'd known what Spears would do..." he stopped talking when Pauly started sobbing again.

"Pa, I took a lot of notes today," Matthew said, "and it isn't confusing to me. Those Indians deserved to die, although doing it in a public square like it was a circus or something probably wasn't right. There must be a better way. Couldn't the doctor just have poisoned them in their jail cells or something like that?"

"That would be cruel," David said. "We wouldn't want to be cruel about it." He looked at Ryker wryly. "It is much more humane to parade them out in front of a half drunk mob and choke them to death."

76

"Well anyway, when we get home I'm going to write this up. Maybe the paper will print it," Matthew said.

"Maybe," David agreed. "Have your mother read it over first."

"I will."

"Okay Lou, it's all over," Calamity Jane said as she and Poker Alice shoved their way into the marshal's office. "I feel naked without my gun." She winked at the deputy. "Although I guess that doesn't feel so bad if there's a handsome man around."

The deputy stepped forward with Jane's pistol in one hand and his shotgun in the other. "Jane, this is your pistol, this is my gun. Mine is for shooting, yours is for fun."

"Why Lou, you're a regular poet," Calamity Jane said. "Let's get married. You can charm me with some of your other verses just like Wild Bill used to do."

"Already married Jane," Louie said. "You know that. But thanks for asking. No other woman has ever proposed to me."

"I'm going to be sick," Poker Alice said. "You two are disgusting."

"Alice, you're just jealous because Lou didn't recite a poem to you," Calamity said. "That was almost as pretty as Bill's poems, Lou."

"You miss Wild Bill Hickok, don't you?" Louie said.

"He was my one true love." Calamity Jane sniffed back a tear. "My Bill!" she wailed.

Alice corrected her none too gently. "Shut up Calam! Wild Bill wasn't yours. He belonged to all of us. He belonged to Deadwood and now that he's gone, he belongs to the ages."

"Say what you will," Calamity Jane replied. "But when my time comes, I'm going to lie right next to him on Mount Moriah. Mark my words on it."

"Calam, you're a dreamer. Anyway, I'm glad that one Injun we just hung won't be fouling our hallowed ground at Mount Moriah," Alice said, lighting a cigar.

"He was a caution, wasn't he?" Louie said. "I'm glad it's over. That poor little boy there with Toby Ryker, why, he got the bejasses scared out of him. Probably have the drizzles for a week."

"They shouldn't let kids that young come to hangings," Poker Alice said. "What was ailing Ryker anyway? I thought he had more sense than that. I'll have to nail the old sidewinder about it the next time I see him."

That evening, Matthew sat alone with his pencil and pad. He was still shaken from the hanging, particularly the curse Dakota Spears placed upon Pauly. He was also curious about that gesture that Grandpa Ryker and Big Nose Charlie exchanged and decided that some day he would ask the old man what that was all about. Glancing at his notes, he decided to tray his hand at reporting what he had just experienced. He wrote in beautiful script like his mother had taught him years ago. He wrote slightly oversize so adults would not have to squint at the fine print.

This past Saturday, accompanied by my grandfather, Toby Ryker, my father, David Stewart, and my little brother Pauly, I attended my first public hanging. It was the hanging of the three Sioux Indians pre-sided over by Marshal Seth Bullock. The hanging was more popular than I guessed it would be. There were all manner of people there, and one group of church ladies led us in song before the festivities began. They were a good choir too, and put everyone in the proper spirit for the occasion.

The executions themselves were as different as the individuals being hung. The first one was of a man named Ron Tuttle. I think his death will haunt me the most. He was very quiet about it and chose not to say anything before dying. I don't know if this was because he simply had nothing to say, or because he felt what he had to say was insignificant, or if he was so disturbed that he couldn't speak even if he wanted to. He seemed like the one of the three who was there only because that is where life placed him. If that is the case, then he was probably dealt a deadly injustice.

The second man who was executed was a man named Dakota Spears. If there is a Hell, then as my grandfather said, even the devil may not want him. He was pure evil. I am inclined to believe that he did the most horrible atrocities that were inflicted upon the families that were killed. I learned from reading the court records that one of the men who was killed tried to fight back and indeed, got a blow in on Spears. For his trouble, Spears wounded him so he couldn't walk and then used his knife to mutilate and scalp him. Spears ended up laughing at the man while he bled to death. If that savage ends up in Hell, then I believe he should suffer that same torture, over and over again. Dakota Spears was also the man who almost started a riot when he put a curse upon my little brother Pauly. I do not know of such things, but I know it disturbed my brother very much and so angered my grandfather that this set the whole crowd off. In the commotion the trap was sprung and Spears ended up dying a prolonged death by strangulation, no doubt adding to the malice his soul already possessed.

The third and next to Ron Tuttle probably the most tragic person in this whole affair was Big Nose Charlie Lamore. He followed the angry, hateful Dakota Spears to the noose, although he was probably the best person to be executed last. I got the feeling from his demeanor that he was the leader of the group. Not only did he apologize to the crowd for Dakota Spears' actions against my brother, but also he successfully wiped him from their hearts. He began with an impersonation of Lincoln, like he was stalling for time, which made everyone laugh. He apologized too, simply but eloquently, for the slayings of the settlers, but said he realized he lived in a white man's world and was willing to accept the judgment passed down upon him. I feel he was next in line to Ron for being dealt a bad hand.

While I may sound like I am praising two of these men, let me point out that I in no way agree with their behavior. They massacred at least two families in ways I have referred to above, including scalping, torture, and burning their homes, sometimes with living people still inside to suffer the horror of the flames.

I will say that I am glad I went to this hanging as it has given me a new appreciation for the consequences that inflicting injustice on others can bring. People who have never seen an execution probably don't think much of hangings one way or the other. Now that I have seen one, I am beginning to understand what my mother means when she says that hanging a prisoner makes us no better than the person we are hanging. In most cases, they have killed another human being, so it becomes a case of an eye for an eye. This explains why the execution was a combination of a religious ceremony as well as a legal, public attraction. On Saturday, people came from miles around to witness three men give their lives to the State and their souls to their God. However, the bible says, Judge not others lest you yourself be judged. I confess that I don't know how that verse from the Good Book squares with what happened on the Deadwood gallows last Saturday afternoon.

In closing, I think it would benefit everyone, whether they agree with it or not, to witness one execution. I don't think a person can adequately pass judgment until seeing everything involved. Signed. Matthew Steven Stewart, Deadwood City.

Setting his pencil aside, Matthew reread what he had written. He figured he would probably make his mother uneasy with his conclusion, but he honestly felt a person should not pass judgment on something without experiencing it. He handed the text to Ida Mae for her opinion as David had suggested and wondered if the paper would print it.

Ida Mae read Matthew's composition quietly. For a long time she said nothing, but he saw her read the article over again twice more while drumming her fingers on the table. Finally she cleared her throat, smiled at him and said, "I'll take this to the newspaper tomorrow."

At bedtime, Pauly lingered with the adults, fearful of going to his room. When Ida Mae finally told him he must get some sleep, he reluctantly went upstairs but began screaming shortly thereafter. David, Ida Mae, and Ryker rushed to his side.

"What is the matter, Pauly?" Ida Mae asked.

"There!" Pauly sobbed, pointing at the darkened window. "He's there!"

The adults looked where Pauly pointed and saw the shadow of a tree limb moving slowly in the breeze that was illuminated by the street lamp outside. Indeed, by applying an overactive imagination, it did look like a man reaching out.

"Pauly, come here," David said, opening the window. "See?" He grabbed the limb and shook it, making the shadow shake as well. "It is just a tree, that's all."

"I'm scared," Pauly said. "That Indian said he'd come in the night when I couldn't see him and he'd kill me. And his ghost got away. You and Grandpa heard it."

"Folks, think I have the answer," Ryker said. "It's in my room. I'll go fetch it." A few minutes later he returned with a leather pouch filled with leaves and earth. "Been carrying this for years Pauly," he said. "It has been blessed by Far Sight Man, my father-in-law and a holy man, and I use it whenever I need to ward off evil spirits. Now Ida Mae, David, stand back a bit while I make the holy circle."

Ida Mae and David did as instructed while Ryker walked around Pauly's bed sprinkling a small amount of the dust on the floor and chanting a lingo that was foreign to them. When he had completely encircled the bed he added, "Oh, and we need to leave a kerosene lamp burnin' low so it isn't dark in here tonight. Evil ghosts don't like it where it is light."

Pauly watched in amazement, the ghost of Dakota Spears totally forgotten as Ryker performed the sacred ritual. Ida Mae and David were equally intrigued. They were not as convinced as Pauly as to the effectiveness of the rite, but they realized that the evil curse of the deceased Indian was imaginary, and if Ryker's magic was more powerful then it would indeed serve the purpose well.

"I must stay here with Pauly tonight," Ryker said. "Just in case this fails, which it has never been known to, I have a few other tricks that will stop an evil ghost in its tracks. Dreamcatchers and such."

The night went without incident as did the second and third nights, which Ryker also spent in Pauly's room to be on the safe side. He felt responsible for the lad's terror and wanted to insure that the harm was undone. It seemed to work, for after the third night nothing more was said on the subject until months later when Pauly brought it up in casual conversation. Then even he was able to laugh about it.

As for Matthew's article, it indeed made an appearance in the paper as a letter to the editor. References upholding Ron Tuttle or Big Nose Charlie Lamore were edited out however. Dakota Territory was not that supportive of the Sioux population whom they viewed as savages.

Deadwood Days

CHAPTER EIGHT

Oh fair and stately maid, whose eye
Was kindled in the upper sky
At the same torch that lighted mine;
For so I must interpret still
Thy sweet dominion o'er my will,
A sympathy divine.

Ah! Let me blameless gaze upon
Features that seem in heart my own,
Nor fear those watchful sentinels
Which charm the more their glance forbids,
Chaste glowing underneath their lids
With fire that draws while it repels.

Laura Stewart read *To Eva,* the Ralph Waldo Emerson poem to herself while lying on her bed that Monday afternoon. The 11-year-old girl was well into a dreamy stage in her life, rich with fantasy of dashing heroes including some dangerous ones like Bobby Parker who were competing for her favor. She never had a real boyfriend and sometimes wondered if she ever would have one, had even cried to her mother about it just last night. She remembered the conversation well.

"Laura, you are a beautiful girl and you will make some lucky young man a fine bride one day."

"I am not a beautiful girl, Mama. I can see what looks back at me in the mirror. I am tall and skinny and my teeth stick out. I have knobby knees. No boy will ever want me."

She remembered how her mother had come to her then and told her that when she was 11 she felt the same way when she looked in the mirror.

"But Mama, you are so pretty," Laura had said. "Matthew and Pauly are even prettier than me even if they are just boys. And I keep getting these dang pimples on my face too! What went wrong anyway?"

"Give yourself time," Ida Mae had said. "You don't think you are pretty, but I do and so does your Papa and even your brothers. And you have a good head and a kind heart too, Laura. You will have plenty of beaus. You'll see."

"And these pigtails!" She remembered shaking her head, causing the long braids to fly every which way. "I hate them! They make me look like a child not a day over nine."

"We can change your hair, Laura," Ida Mae had said. "Maybe we should comb it out tonight and try it that way for a while if it would make you feel better."

"Can we, Mama?"

"Certainly."

Laura closed her dream world of Mister Emerson, sighed, and went downstairs to see what her mother was doing. Ida Mae was just arising from the couch as she entered the parlor.

"Mama, are you all right?" Laura asked.

"Yes, I was just resting my eyes a bit," Ida Mae said. "I had a hint of a headache after classes were over. I may need reading spectacles. It's gone now."

"Let's go do something, Mama."

Ida Mae looked outside. "It was overcast earlier but it seems to be clearing off. All right, let's us ladies go uptown. We can shop a bit. I would like a new dress and as much as you have grown lately, you could use a new one for church too."

"You've always made my dresses before, Mama."

"I know, but sometimes it's fun to treat ourselves, and I think we deserve it," Ida Mae said. "Come on."

The Stewart women spent the next two hours shopping. They tried on the fashions of the day, from hats to dresses to shoes, searching the stores for a wardrobe that flattered them both. For those few hours, mother and daughter enjoyed being high society ladies of Deadwood.

"Let's see here, Hiram T. Custis, Seth said his name was, and he has an office along here somewheres." Ryker glanced at the storefronts and the signs above them as he walked up the main street of Deadwood. Crossing the street, he happened to spot the shingle toward the rear of a building. "Ah, there he is, by golly."

Entering the small office, Ryker was greeted by an older woman whom he learned was the lawyer's wife, legal assistant, and typist. "Mister Custis is at the courthouse just now," she said, looking Ryker over. He will be back in about an hour and can see you then, Mister..."

"Ryker, ma'am, Toby Ryker's my handle," he said, removing his hat and making a slight bow.

"Well, Mister Ryker, you are welcome to have a seat and wait or you can come back."

Ryker saw Ida Mae and Laura pass by on the street as Mrs. Custis spoke. "I believe I will come back. Thank you, ma'am," Once outside, he snuck up behind Ida Mae and Laura and deliberately bumped into them. "Hey, you two slowpokes, shake your tail feathers," he bellowed.

The ladies didn't bother to turn, recognizing the sound of Ryker's voice. "Sounds like a mugger behind us," Ida Mae said loudly.

"He probably wants all our jewels," Laura answered.

"Actually, I just would like the pleasure of your company," Ryker said. "Being in the company of two such looksome women on such a fine day makes an old man feel sprightly."

Ryker and the women walked and gossiped, enjoying the day and each other's friendship. He accompanied them as they modeled clothing and gave his approval to the items they selected, insisting on paying for them out of his poke. "Ain't often I get to splurge on even one such a lovely lady to say nothing about two."

"Thank you Grandpa," Laura said, kissing him.

"No, thank *you*," Ryker said.

"For what?"

"Just for being you," Ryker said. "And for adopting this ornery old cuss."

"You aren't nearly as ornery as you want people to believe you are," Laura said. As she spoke, a boy about her age walked by and looked her over, smiling shyly. "He smiled at me, Mama!"

"Imagine that," Ida Mae said, winking at Ryker.

The pleasant hour passed too quickly and Ryker had to excuse himself and return to the office of attorney Hiram T. Custis while Ida Mae and Laura walked on home. "Mister Custice is in his office now," Mrs. Custis said as Ryker entered. "You can go right in."

"Hiram Thaddeus Custis at your service," said the rotund attorney as he stood and offered his hand. "Here, would you like a peppermint?"

"Don't think so," Ryker said, shaking hands with the lawyer. "They give me gas."

"They're supposed to do just the opposite."

"Yeah, well anyway, Marshal Bullock said I should tell you my story. I'm the guy that shot Billy Brump about two years back."

"William Krump."

"Huh?"

"His name was William Krump not Billy Brump, Mister Ryker."

"Doggone it all, I always get his name mixed up."

"The Peoples Bank case. I remember it well. In fact, I drew up the complaint against you. What did you do that for, for cripes sake?"

Ryker proceeded to explain in full detail the story of the hide cutters and that tragic day in the Pawnee camp when his life was changed forever. "I never forgot that man, Mister Custis. And when I seen him here in Deadwood two years back, the memories all came back to me like it happened yesterday. That's when I shot him and I don't regret it. I hear his wife and daughter are going without since he died though and that I do regret. It wasn't their doings what happened in that Pawnee camp."

"Yes, Esmeralda and Camille are on hard times," the attorney said.

"I'd like to do something about that," Ryker said. "I have the means."

"That would be a grand gesture but you certainly are not obligated," Custice replied.

"I know I'm not," but it wasn't their fault old Willy was a snake, and they shouldn't have to suffer on account of what he did."

"Let me look up the law, Mister Ryker. I will also check on the assault charge against you here in town. Even though it is a minor offense, it is still on the books and we should take care of that."

"That would be grand," Ryker said. "I don't think of myself as a criminal. Talked to Marshal Bullock about it and he said he'd let me go on my own renaissance."

"Recognizance," Custis corrected him.

"Yeah, what you said. Anyway, I don't have to dig into my poke and post no bail money until all this is settled."

"Very well. I will try to arrange a meeting with Esmeralda and Camille and you and me," Hiram said. "It's called an arbitration conference. We'll get started on sorting all this out."

"They probably hate me," Ryker replied.

"They might, I don't know," Hiram said. "They certainly are under no obligation to meet with us, but there is no harm in asking them."

"Okay, if you think so," Ryker said, arising. "I'd be obliged if you'd post me a note at the Stewart place when you know something,"

"I'll leave word for you there. It will be a few weeks."

"What do I owe you?"

"Nothing right now," the attorney said. "My wife Prudence keeps track of all that. We'll bill you when it's all over."

"Well, it's been my pleasure so have a pleasant day," Ryker said, heading toward the door.

"Matthew, I'm having an engineer from the mining school in Lead come over here and check our property," David said.

"Why, dad?" Matthew replied, setting down the wheelbarrow on his return trip from the flume at the Potato Creek Mine.

"Because I think there's a better way to mine than the way we are doing it, that's why. Now Stumpy's gone, but neither he nor Toby knew that much about hard rock mining anyway. It just seems to me there is a better way to do this, but I don't know that much about it either." David nodded at his son. "That's why I invested the money to have a consultant come in here."

"If you say so dad," Matthew said. "But geez, we're taking darn near a hundred dollars a day out of the place."

"Yes and probably throwing another hundred away into Potato Creek in the gold that is embedded in quartz rock," David said. "That doesn't make sense to me."

"Suppose you are right," Matthew said. "Say dad, do you have a minute to talk about something else?"

"Sure. Let's go inside."

When father and son were seated in the office, Matthew spelled it out. "You know Becky Brown and I have been seeing each other on a regular basis."

"I gathered that," David said.

"I love her, dad," Matthew said. "We'd like to get married."

"That would be grand," David said. "Becky is a wonderful woman and would be a great addition to our family. Have you talked to her folks about it yet?"

"No, we haven't gotten that far yet," Matthew said.

"That is the honorable thing to do," David said. "With our new house being ready to move into next week, you two can move into the rental."

"I wasn't expecting that. Thanks, dad."

"You'd better tell her parents also," David said. You don't want to elope and start out a marriage having your in-laws down on you."

"True. I'll go out there tonight after work."

After completing his shift, Matthew rushed home but was too excited to sit down with the family for supper. He hurriedly gulped down a sandwich, cleaned up, changed clothes, and headed out to the barn where he saddled Wino and was off to Becky Brown's house. When he arrived, she was coming in from the garden.

"Becky! I talked to Pa today and guess what? He's going to let us have the house."

"The house! That's, wonderful," Becky said. "I worried about where we would live."

"They are all set to move next week and the rent on the place is cheap. With what I make at the mine, we can handle it easy."

They embraced. "This is so wonderful, Matthew."

"Just think, if I hadn't moved to Deadwood none of this would be happening."

"No, it wouldn't," Becky said.

"I want to formally ask your folks for your hand."

"Well, now is a good time. The boys are out and about doing heaven knows what, and Papa and Mama are both to home." Becky took his hand. "Let's go in."

Once Matthew entered the Brown house, shyness overcame him. What if Mister Brown said he couldn't have Becky? His nervousness increased as he entered the parlor where Axel Brown, a muscular blacksmith, was reading the paper.

"Hi, Papa," Becky said. "Matthew has something to say to you."

Axel peered over his paper at his daughter and Matthew. "I heard you come galloping up, Matthew Stewart," he said, putting the paper aside. "What is it?"

By now, Matthew's heart was slamming in his chest, and he lost his nerve. "Um, isn't it a lovely day? I sure enjoyed the ride out here."

"I'm sure you did, but I doubt you rode all the way from your place to tell me what a fine day it is."

"No, sir, I didn't," Matthew said. He looked at Becky then back at her father. "I came out here to ask for your daughter's hand in marriage and for your blessing."

"You can't have her."

"What?"

"Just kidding. Relax, Matthew Stewart," Axel Brown said, throwing back his head and roaring with hearty laughter. "Mother, come on in here!"

Lucille Brown, wiping some flour on her apron, entered from the kitchen. "What is it Axel? Oh, hello Matthew, it is good to see you. Have you had supper?"

"Just a ham sandwich, Mrs. Brown."

"Psshtt," Lucille said, pursing her lips and shoving Matthew with her hand. "A miner can't live on that. We're having roast pork and dumplings. I'll set an extra plate."

"Matthew wants you to be his mother-in-law, dear," Axel said.

"I gathered that from what Becky has been telling me," Lucille said. "Are you a church-going man?"

"Lutheran."

"Then I'd be honored."

"So, when do you two plan to tie the knot and start working on giving us some grandchildren we can spoil," Axel said.

"Oh, Pa," Becky said, blushing.

"Yes Axel, I think you're rushing things a bit," Lucille said. "Unless…Rebecca, you aren't…"

"No Ma, I'm not pregnant."

"We would like to get married next week," Matthew said. "I love your daughter very much and I can't wait to make her my wife."

Axel and Lucille were silent, holding hands as Matthew and Becky kissed chastely. "That's fine with us," Axel said. "But on such short notice it will be a small wedding."

"Fine," Becky said. "We just want the two families and Reverend Lancaster in attendance anyway."

"It's settled then," Axel said as the four boys, Jerome, James, Jeremiah, and John, came rushing into the house. "Boys, you sister is getting married. Now clean up and head out to the table for supper."

"If Becky gets married, who's going to help Mama with the house chores?" John, the youngest, asked.

"Why, you will," Axel said. "You will become our girl. We'll start calling you Joanna instead of John. You'll look so pretty in a dress."

"Axel, don't tease John in front of company," Lucille said.

"Who's teasing?" Axel said.

As the family headed out to the dinner table, Lucille leaned over to Matthew. "Sometimes I wonder about that old coot."

"He doesn't mean it, does he?" Matthew whispered.

"Who knows?" Becky said. "You wouldn't think anybody would seriously think about raising skunks and making hats out of their fur either, would you?"

Matthew motioned over his shoulder at Axel "You mean –"

"Um-hum. Right now there are six skunk caps hanging in the closet."

CHAPTER NINE

"Easy does it now, Wino." Ryker led the quarter horse gelding around in a large circle to the right while Matthew, walking behind, pulled gently on the right rein. They were teaching the gelding to drive. Smart horse; it took to the driving harness without complaint. It leaned its weight into the breast collar and pulled, dragging the fence post that was log-chained to the tugs. The men worked with the horse less than a half hour and already it demonstrated it was ready for a singletree and a buckboard.

"Do you suppose Wino can pull Becky and my wedding carriage, Grandpa? " Matthew asked. "He's like one of the family. I'd like that."

"I'm sure he could Matthew," Ryker said. "Like you, he's dependable. Where are you and the lovely Miss Becky going for your honeymoon?"

"We're going down to Rapid City," Matthew said. "We can watch some plays."

"And?" Ryker said.

"And, of course, there are some great restaurants there, so we're told," Matthew said.

"And?"

"And we might look around for some new furniture for the house, and some new tack for Wino, and maybe even get some ideas for Papa Brown to build us a new Sunday carriage."

'And!"

Matthew smiled. "And we probably will spend some time in the hotel doing a lot of loving."

'Well, I should hope so!" Ryker said, slapping Matthew on the back and laughing. "I wish you kids all the best. You deserve it." He handed a deed to Matthew. "And you don't need to pay rent on that house. It's yours."

"Grandpa Ryker," Matthew said. "What is this?"

"The deed to the house. It's yours. I want to give it to you and Becky as a wedding gift, and proud I am that I can do it for you too. If I was to have a real live grandson by blood, I'd want him to be just like you, Matthew. You make a granddad proud." Ryker got tears in his eyes.

"Aw Grandpa," Matthew said as he hugged the old man. "If I had a real live granddad, I'd want him to be just like you too." He stepped back. "But Grandpa, giving me Wino, helping me train him, buying the house for me and Becky, and I heard from Pa and Ma you are seeing a lawyer…are you fixing to do something?"

"You have wisdom beyond your years," Ryker said. "Let's just say I'm putting things in order."

"Whatever that means," Matthew said.

"One day you will understand," Ryker said. The two men hugged again. "Let's run Wino through his paces one more time."

"Mister Stewart, you have a rich claim, here," Joshua Pickles said. The engineer from the School of Mines in Lead took notes as he and David walked through the main shaft of the Potato Creek Mine. "But your mining methods are archaic. You need a stamp mill to break down this quartz. There is so much gold here that you are passing by."

"That's what I figured. How expensive is a stamp mill?" David asked.

"Like any modern equipment, it is not cheap," Pickles replied. "But I can assure you that with the additional recovery you will obtain, the equipment will pay for itself in short order."

"How much mine life do I have here if I implement modern methods?" David asked.

"I'd say just based on what I see here, at least ten years," Pickles said. "My guess is that with additional core samples, the mine life will be considerably more than that." He looked hard at David. "You have a million dollars in resources here, Mister Stewart."

"A million dollars?"

"Yes sir, conservatively."

"I have a hard time even thinking in those terms. How much will it cost me to extract it?"

"With the proper equipment and labor costs, about forty cents on the dollar. This is a rich mine."

"Can you write that up for me so the bank will lend me the money?"

"That I can Mister Stewart, and would be most happy to."

The following week was a busy one for the Stewarts. They moved into their new stone two-story home on Tuesday and on Friday, Matthew married Becky Brown at the Our Savior's Lutheran church in Deadwood. Toby Ryker was Matthew's best man and Laura Stewart was Becky's bridesmaid. Jeremiah Brown knew how to strum a guitar so he and his brothers sang a few hymns during the service. They let Pauly stand with them and hold a hymnal although he was a bit too shy to sing in public. The Brown boys weren't particularly good at it, but like Lucille said, it was the thought that counted.

"They make such a handsome couple up there," Ida Mae said to David as Matthew and Becky prepared to exchange their vows. The boys began to sing *Bringing in the Sheaves*.

"That is the first suit Matthew's ever owned," David said. "You picked a nice color, Ida Mae."

"Black goes with anything." She touched at a tear. "It seems like just yesterday he was a baby."

"He is a fine young man," David said. "He's done us proud."

"They make such a lovely couple don't they, Axel?" Lucille said.

"Dang cummerbund...oh, yes dear, yes, they certainly do. And our boys...well, they are them."

"Becky, our eldest," Lucille said. "It seems like just yesterday she was a baby."

"She's been a fine daughter to be sure, my dear. She's done us proud."

"That's my wedding dress, Axel."

"I know," Axel said as he and Lucille joined the Stewarts with the refrain:

Bringing in the sheaves, bringing in the sheaves
We shall come rejoicing, bringing in the sheaves.

"Dearly beloved," Reverend Lancaster began, "we are gathered here today in the sight of God and this company to join these two young people in holy matrimony." He looked at Axel and Lucille. "Who giveth this woman?"

"We do," Axel and Lucille said.

"And who giveth this man?"

"We do," David and Ida Mae said.

"Does anyone here present have cause to object to this holy union?" Reverend Lancaster said. "If so, speak now or forever hold your peace." The small church was silent.

He turned to Matthew. "Matthew Steven Stewart, do you take Rebecca Angela Brown as your lawful wedded wife, to have and to hold, for better, for worse, for richer, for poorer, in sickness and in health, until death do you part?"

"I do," Matthew said.

Reverend Lancaster nodded to Becky. "Rebecca Angela Brown, do you take Matthew Steven Stewart as your lawful wedded husband, to have and to hold, for better, for worse, in sickness and in health, until death do you part?"

"I do," Becky said.

"Very well then, by the authority vested in me, I hereby pronounce you man and wife. What God has joined together, let no man put asunder." He turned to Laura. "And now, Laura Stewart wishes to read a poem which she has dedicated to the newly married couple. Laura?"

Laura stepped forward and stood next to Reverend Lancaster facing her brother and sister-in-law, Ryker, the choir of the Browns and Pauly, and the two sets of parents. "This is for you, Matthew and Becky," she said. "I think it speaks of the love you have for one another as you begin your life together. It is by Elizabeth Barrett Browning." She unfolded a paper.

"How do I love thee? Let me count the ways.

94

I love thee to the depth and breath and height
My soul can reach, when feeling out of sight
For the ends of being and ideal grace.
I love thee to the level of everyday's
Most quiet need, by sun and candle-light.
I love thee freely, as men strive for right;
I love thee purely, as they turn from praise.
I love thee with a passion put to use
In my old griefs, and with my childhood's faith.
I love thee with a faith I seemed to lose
With my lost saints, I love thee with the breath,
Smiles, tears, of all my life! And if God choose,
I shall but love thee better after death."

Folding the paper, she returned to her place next to the bridal couple. The church was silent as all reflected on the words of this simple gift said from the heart of a young girl to her brother and new sister-in-law. Everyone from Toby Ryker on down wiped their eyes.

"That was beautiful Miss Stewart," Reverend Lancaster said. "Thank you for sharing that with us today. And now friends," he motioned for Matthew and Becky to turn toward their parents, "I present you with Mister and Missus Matthew Stewart."

The Brown boys began to belt out *A Mighty Fortress Is Our God*, which even Pauly joined in on as Matthew and Becky, followed by Ryker, Laura, Mr. and Mrs. Brown and Mr. and Mrs. Stewart filed out of the church into the warm sunshine outside. The group chatted briefly and shook hands all around then made straightaway for the Brown residence for punch, wedding cake, and a light lunch.

"We want to start a singing group," Jeremiah said, sipping from his punch cup.

"Yeah," John said. "We already know a few hymns and we can sing *The Streets of Larado.*"

"Well, you'll need more than that if you want people to pay to listen to you sing," Matthew said.

"And you need something livelier than hymns that people can dance to," Becky said.

"Now Becky," Lucille said, "you know I've always frowned on dancing. Life is meant to be but a vale of tears."

"Mother, times are changing," Axel said. "We have to change with them. Boys, I think you should write your own songs. Maybe something along the ballad line, some sad but some lively. Love songs are always good. Have a lead singer, probably Jeremiah because he has the best voice."

"What would the rest of us do?" Jerome said.

"Yeah," John said. "Stand around and look stupid?"

"You do a pretty good job of that anyway," Axel said, laughing.

"Pa," James said, pouting.

"Now seriously boys, I think the three of you should be backup singers to Jeremiah."

"Backup singers? What's that?" Matthew asked.

"I've never heard of it," Becky said.

"Well, a backup singer stands in the background and harmonizes with the lead singer," Axel explained patiently. "The way I have this worked out in my head, you boys should try something really different. While Jeremiah is singing, you should dance in unison, maybe put your feet out and back and your arms out and back and spin around once in a while and snap your fingers and say things like 'ooh yeah' and 'wa-wa-wa' and 'shooby-doo.'"

Ryker was listening in and started snapping his fingers. "Think you got something there, Axel."

The two men began to say 'wa-wa-wa' then locked arms and twirled one another square dance style. The four Brown boys stared at the two men as Becky and Matthew chuckled. Lucille shook her head and wandered off to the Stewart family and Reverend Lancaster with some mints, the sound of her thick elevated heals clacking loudly on the pine floor.

"Pa, did you fall out of bed this morning and bump your noggin?" Jeremiah said.

"Geez, we try doing anything like that and folks will shoot at us," Jerome said.

"That or run us out of town," John added.

James just rolled his eyes and also wandered over toward the Stewarts.

"They need a catchy name," Ryker said. "How about the Brown Spots, their last name being Brown."

"Yeah," Axel said. "They can sew some across their butts." Ryker and Axel wandered toward the door. "That, or the Jay Birds, since all their names start with 'J'," Axel mused aloud. "They can dress in prison stripes."

"Course, on the other hand, maybe the boys are right," Ryker said. "They start talking that gibberish, folks might think they're touched in the head. Might try and put them in one of them there insane asylums or something."

"Maybe, but it doesn't sound any more stupid than yodeling."

"Ya got me there," Ryker said.

Matthew and Becky headed over toward Reverend Lancaster and the other group. "Ma, Pa, Laura, Pauly, Mrs. Brown," Matthew said, shaking hands with them all, "Mrs. Stewart and I will be on our way." He also shook hands with the preacher. "Reverend Lancaster, thank you for marrying us today. Folks, I'm so happy you could share this with us."

"That goes for me, too," Becky said.

"My best wishes to you both," Reverend Lancaster said. "I hope to see you in church on Sundays. And when you get back from Rapid City, stop by and I'll sign you up for the tithing program."

"I'll take the rest of the cake and the gifts to the house," Ida Mae said. "They will be waiting for you upon your return."

"Maybe not the cake," Pauly said.

After hugs and kisses were exchanged all around, the bridal couple waved at the Brown boys, said their goodbyes to Axel and Ryker, and climbed aboard the white carriage they had rented for the occasion. Matthew slapped the reins to Wino and they were off to Rapid City. They had an enjoyable honeymoon, savoring not only the sights and sounds of the city, but the intimate bliss of each other's company during the long, romantic nights in the hotel. All too soon the young couple returned to Deadwood and settled into the domestic routine of husband and wife.

A month later, the new equipment was installed in the Potato Creek Mine. Joshua Pickles oversaw the installation of it and taught David,

Matthew, Frankie Malone, and the other two miners David hired how to operate the new equipment. His prediction was soon proven correct; the mine's production increased many times over within a short time.

"This is better than I had hoped Matthew," David said, looking over the ledgers. "Our deposits are skyrocketing. This equipment will be paid for in no time."

"That's good," Matthew said. "It will feel good to have that bank loan paid off. And I would like to request a raise." He smiled. "Becky and I are expecting a baby."

"So soon?" David shook his son's hand. "Congratulations to both of you. This is wonderful, and of course a raise is in order. I intended to do that anyway and also to make you part owner in the mine. That way, you will receive dividends."

"Thanks dad. I appreciate it."

"There's something else. Matthew, I want you to take some classes at the mining school in Lead. We need to know more about modern mining than we do. We are just lucky we are on the receiving end of Toby Ryker's generosity here, but from now on it is up to us to develop this mine."

"I agree," Matthew said. "And I'll gladly take some classes."

The next afternoon, Pauly and Chen Wong, his Chinese friend, hid behind some tombstones in Mount Moriah cemetery watching the Chinese burial service that was taking place there. Chen was one of numerous Chinese children in Deadwood whose parents, besides providing cheap labor in the mines, also worked as domestics within the town.

"We can go in there if we want to," Chen said. "They won't care."

"But, I'm not Chinese," Pauly said.

"You are with me," Chen said. "It will be all right. And look at all that food! We have a feast when we honor our dead."

"Just the same, I'd rather wait," Pauly said.

"Tell you what, I'll go over there and get us some food and then…" Chen put his hand to his mouth to stifle a smile, "we'll sneak back to your house and eat it!"

"Now you are talking," Pauly said. "We got milk."

"What about your mom?"

"Oh yeah, I forgot about her. I'll sneak the pitcher out of the icebox, and we can hide in the barn and eat. She'll never find us."

"Okay," Chen said, heading toward the funeral crowd. Just then firecrackers began to explode, signaling that the body of the deceased was being lowered into the ground. Chen looked back at Pauly and grinned.

"Got some roast pig here, and some goose and some sugar cakes," he said upon his return. "Let's go." The two boys wound their way through the tombstones to the Stewart house.

"You go in the horse stalls," Pauly said. "I'll be right out with the milk and some plates."

"Don't forget a couple forks," Chen said. Don't bring chopsticks. I don't like eating with those dumb things."

"I don't have any chopsticks anyway."

A few moments later, Chen saw Pauly balancing a milk pitcher on two plates and heading toward the barn. He disappeared into one of the horse stalls.

"Chen?"

"In this one," Chen said.

"Help me with this."

Chen took the milk pitcher from Pauly then scurried back into the horse stall followed by his friend.

"I didn't bring cups," Pauly said.

"We can both drink right out of the pitcher."

"Yeah, so long as Ma isn't looking. She hates it when I do that. Says it's unsanitary or some dumb thing like that."

"Pauly Stewart! Who is in there with you?" Ida Mae hollered.

"I thought she didn't see you," Chen said.

"I thought so too. I never saw her. Hi, Mom!" Pauly hollered back. "It's just me and Chen."

"Come out here this instant. And bring that food with you. There is no need to hide in a barn and eat like animals."

By the time Chen and Pauly left the barn with their feast, both Ida Mae and Laura were on the back porch watching them.

"Did you steal that from the funeral service?" Ida Mae demanded.

"Well, not exactly," Chen said. "We just took some. The funeral was for my uncle Chow."

"Good name." Pauly grinned, but neither Ida Mae nor Laura smiled back so he stopped smiling too.

"That is so pathetic," Laura said, looking down her nose at Pauly. "Stealing food from a funeral!"

"Oh, go read a poem or something," Pauly huffed.

"Mother!"

"Go on inside Laura," Ida Mae said. "I'll handle this."

After Laura left, she said, "Well boys, come on into the kitchen. I tend to forget how boys your age are always hungry, and I guess it is all right, the honorable Mister Chow being your relative as he was. I do recall hearing of his passing."

The boys enjoyed a leisurely snack, albeit a large one, with Ida Mae who sat with them and listened to Chen speak of his uncle and of their life in Deadwood. Chen's father, Lei Wong, was looking for work and Ida Mae thought David might have a position available for him at the mine since the man had mining experience. After a pleasant hour the boys departed for yet another adventure or two before suppertime.

Ida Mae returned to the parlor to find Laura sobbing. "Laura, what is the matter?"

"It's Bobby Parker, Mama. The Deadwood paper says a train was robbed in Telluride Colorado a few weeks back. The way they describe it just like when we came here to Deadwood, I'm sure it was him."

"Let me see that, Laura." Ida Mae took the paper from her daughter, scanned the headlines, and read the brief article. "You are right. It sounds like Bobby."

"Why does he do it Mama? Grandpa Ryker is right. He'll die bloody."

"I don't know Laura. We don't know for sure it is Bobby. Let's pray it isn't."

"I could have loved him, Mama."

This was one time the power of prayer would fail the Stewart women. The newspapers would remind them time and time again over the next several years that indeed Bobby Parker, aka Butch Cassidy, had become an outlaw. He and the Sundance Kid and their gang, the Wild Bunch, would live to commit robberies of banks and trains for many years to come. While he became a Robin Hood type legend to countless people, he never realized he stopped being a romantic hero to a young girl he met but twice along the way – once in a swing station in Wyoming, and several months later on a train winding its way to Deadwood in the Dakota Territory.

CHAPTER TEN

"Glad you could make it, Mister Ryker," Hiram Custice said.

"I got to thinking about your name," Ryker replied. "Ain't that a Civil War name?"

"The name Custis dates to the Civil War and before, yes," Hiram said. "I am of that lineage. In fact, Arlington National Cemetery is built on Custis ground."

"Thought so," Ryker said. "You got any children to carry on your name?"

"Nope, the wife's barren. All Prudence and I have for kin is a stupid calico cat we call Bella Sue." Hiram leaned toward Ryker and whispered, "We named her after the Bella Union." He looked around. "There she is. We let her come downstairs from the apartment sometimes."

Ryker looked at the cat which lay on its back on a rug dozing in a patch of sunlight. "Bella Sue, huh?"

"Yeah, she's a house cat. A big tub of lard like us. Likes to eat. Sits right up at the table and begs for food. I hate that. Prudence indulges her though."

"Folks grow fond of their pets," Ryker said. "I had a horse. Name's Wino because he likes a nip now 'n then. Gave him to the eldest Stewart boy."

"The one who just got married a while back? I heard about that."

"That's the one. Married into the Brown family. Axel Brown."

"Axel Brown." Hiram chuckled. "Now there's a dreamer."

"Yeah, he's a character all right," Ryker said. "But he's a good old boy. His wife Lucille wears her corset a bit too tight to suit me though."

"Yes, Lucille thoroughly enjoys being miserable. Anyway, Bella our cat sheds hair all over the dang house."

"Cats do that," Ryker said. "She ever make you sneeze?"

"Yes, sometimes," Hiram said. "How'd you know?"

"Well, because I know sometimes cats fur makes some people sneeze, that's all," Ryker said. "And makes their eyes puddle up."

"Most times I just get her fur all over my suits. She sleeps in my chair, the dumb thing."

"You wouldn't trade her for the world though, would you?"

"Naw, guess not," Hiram said, smiling. "Well, you've heard all about me for free. Now let's talk about you on your dime. I met with Esmeralda Krump. She is very willing to meet with us for an arbitration conference."

"She will?" Ryker said, surprised.

"Yes she will, and her daughter Camille too," Hiram said. "Surprised me also."

He glanced at his appointment book. How does next Monday at ten o'clock sound?"

"Sounds fine to me," Ryker said. "What will I say? What will I do?"

"Just tell them your story like you told me," Hiram said. "About how you came to shoot Willy Krump. Esmeralda may want to tell you a few things too."

"Sounds fair enough," Ryker said. "But I got to tell you that this will be hard for me. Every time I tell this tale, I relive it," he took out a handkerchief and dabbed at his eyes, "and my wife and daughter have to die all over again. Every time that happens, a piece of me dies too."

Hiram said nothing for a moment, just looked soberly at Ryker until the old man regained his composure. "I'm sure it is difficult," he said softly. "But maybe we can put this to rest for once and for all. I hope so, for all concerned."

"I hope so too," Ryker said, standing up. "Hiram, thank you, and I'll see you come Monday."

Ryker had barely stepped outside the Custis Law Office when he heard a bell ringing and an awful commotion toward Main Street. Heading that direction, he saw the fire hose cart drawn by two horses racing down the street toward the saloons. Glancing skyward, he saw billowing black smoke coming from the roof of the Bodega Bar. When he arrived, Ida Mae, Pauly, Laura, Becky, and Chen were viewing the flames that threatened to engulf the entire building.

"Howdy folks," Ryker said. "Best step back from that roof. Them sparks can fly off there and burn you."

Ida Mae drew the children back. "Yes Toby, you are correct."

"I wonder what started it Grandpa," Pauly said.

"Probably Poker Alice's cigar," Toby joked. "Speaking of Alice, there she is."

Poker Alice made her way through the crowd that had gathered and approached him. "Ryker, you dumb old jackass." She was about to lay into him for bringing Pauly to the hanging, but then she noticed the family and blushed.

"No need to by shy Alice," Ryker said. "Come on over here and meet my family."

"No Ryker, I can't. They're decent folks. I –"

"And so are you," Ryker said, guiding her by the arm. "Ida Mae, Becky, Laura, Pauly, Chen, I want you to meet a very dear friend of mine, Poker Alice. She's the best poker player in Deadwood and has a heart of gold to match it."

"Alice," Ida Mae said, shaking her hand.

"Actually, it's Alice Tubbs, ma'am."

"I'm Ida Mae to my friends, Alice. And if you are a friend of Grandpa Ryker then you are a friend of mine."

Poker Alice looked surprised. "Grandpa Ryker?"

"Yes, we've adopted him," Laura said.

Alice gave up her idea of chastising Ryker and smiled at the assembly. "Chen, I know you. How's your mama?"

"Fine," Chen said. "I don't see her much. She keeps house for the rich folks now days. She just started working for Dora and Joseph Du-Fran."

"The DuFrans, huh?" She raised her eyebrows at Ryker, wondering if he had met the brothel madam. "And what do you do all day, Chen?"

"I go to Missus Stewart's school with Pauly," Chen said. "We learn a lot of stuff."

"That's nice of you, Missus Stewart," Alice said.

"I like to help out where I can," Ida Mae said. "Chen's father Lei just started working at our mine."

"That's right, the Potato Creek," Alice said.

An explosion rocked the fire-ridden building as several kegs of whiskey stored on the second floor overheated and burst.

"Clear the area you folks," a fireman hollered. "Quit your gawking and lollygagging. You want to get burned up?"

"Let's go back to the house," Ryker said. "We're just in the way here."

Poker Alice went her own way after bidding the family adieu and Ryker and the others retired to the Stewart mansion, for in a town of shacks and clapboard houses and even tents, a mansion was what it was. Ida Mae put some water in the teakettle.

"Pauly, you and Chen can play ball in the yard for a half hour," she said. "But don't wander back to that fire." She motioned at Laura. "Laura, you go outside too. The fresh air will do you good."

"Okay Mama," Pauly said.

"Can we have cookies then?" Chen said. "You make good cookies, Missus Stewart."

"I think that can be arranged."

"Mama, do I have to go out with them?" Laura whined. "I'd rather stay in the house with you and Grandpa Ryker."

"No, you go out too. Take a book and sit on the garden bench if you like, but go."

"Oh, all right," Laura grumped, picking up a book and heading toward the boys.

"Just stay out of our way, you ninny," Pauly said, sticking his tongue out at Laura.

"See what I mean?" Laura said.

"Pauly, be nice to your sister."

"Why? She isn't nice to me."

"Pauly, apologize."

"But –"

"Apologize."

"Oh, all right. I'm sorry, Laura."

"Now all of you out of here! Scoot!" Ida Mae said, waving them away.

"Okay, let's go," Chen said. "Last one to the barn is a rotten egg!"

After the children were gone, Ida Mae fixed Ryker a cup of tea. "Toby, where were you today?"

"Met with Hiram Custis, my lawyer," Ryker said. "It's about the shooting."

"I hope you can get that settled and off your mind," Ida Mae said.

"Me too Sarge," Ryker said. "He's scheduled what he calls an arbitration conference for next Monday. It's with Willy Krump's next of kin. That's the heathen I shot."

"It sounds stressful," Ida Mae said. "Would you like me to come along?"

"Thanks Sarge but no. This deal was of my making and I want to settle it myself."

"All right, if you say so. By the way, isn't it wonderful that Matthew and Becky are expecting a baby?"

"Yes and so soon. My gosh Sarge, that's another generation of Stewarts already."

"Another generation. It doesn't seem possible Toby. Where does the time go?"

"Flies by," Ryker said. "And the older you get the faster it flies. But you can be real proud of Matthew and Becky. Matthew, working hard there in the mine and soon to be a daddy. And Becky, such a pretty young thing, so kind, so gentle, they will make great parents. And a lot of that is because of how you and David and the Browns raised them, Sarge. You did an admirable job. I could have done no better even if I had the chance."

Ida Mae rubbed Ryker's shoulders "You still think about Wild Flower and Hope don't you? Even after all these years."

Ryker set the teacup down, took Ida Mae's hand, and kissed it. "There isn't a day what goes by, Ida Mae," he said as his eyes grew wet with tears. "There isn't a day."

Laura was reading Elizabeth Barrett Browning as she sat on the garden bench, the sound of Pauly and Chen hollering at each other fading into the background. She sensed someone's presence and looked up to see a boy about her size smiling at her.

"Hello," he said. "I'm Ethan Lattimore. We live three houses down."

"Hi," Laura said back. He had the bluest eyes she had ever seen, curly brown hair, and eyelashes that would be the envy of any girl. "Have you lived here long?"

"Was born here," Ethan said, jumping over the picket fence and sitting next to her. "My dad owns the freight line between here and Rapid City. We haul a lot of the gold out and a lot of the supplies in."

"How exciting," Laura said. She felt her toes start to tingle. "My dad owns the Potato Creek Mine. Your dad probably hauls some of our gold to Rapid City. We have accounts there."

"I bet we do," Ethan said. "Unless he hauls it himself, it goes by Lattimore Dray Line."

"My Mama is starting a school in our house. Would you like to come?"

"Yeah, sure. I can add things up a little bit but I can't read much."

"We, um, my mother can teach you," Laura said. "It's really easy and fun too." She scooted next to him. "See this book? It has poems in it. This one is by Elizabeth Barrett Browning. I read it at my brother's wedding. It starts like this." She moved her finger under each word as she recited the poem.

> How do I love thee? Let me count the ways.
> I love thee to the depth and breath and height
> My soul can reach, when feeling out of sight
> For the ends of being and ideal grace.

Looking into those blue, blue eyes, she smiled and he smiled back. "See? It's easy," she chirped.

"Ye-yeah," Ethan stammered, still staring at Laura. "You have pretty hair."

"Thank you," she giggled. A ball came flying in and bounced off the bench, startling them. "Pauly!"

Ida Mae opened the back door just in time to see the happenings at the garden bench. "Pauly, Chen, it is time to come in now. Laura...oh, hello, who is your friend?"

Ethan accompanied Laura to the door and even carried her book of verse. "Mama, this is our neighbor, Ethan Lattimore. His daddy runs the dray line to Rapid City. He'd like to come to your school!"

"Laura, my recruiter." Ida Mae laughed. "Ethan, I would love to have you in my school. I plan to place an ad in the paper this very week and for two weeks hereafter to see what type of response I receive. Besides Chen and my daughter-in-law, you will be my third student."

"Thanks ma'am," Ethan said. "I'm grateful."

"Step inside," Ida Mae said. "You can get started today."

After classes were over and Becky, Ethan, and Chen returned to their homes, Laura joined Ida Mae in the kitchen.

"Oh, Mama, isn't Ethan wonderful? He said I have nice hair!"

Ida Mae looked hard at her daughter. "Now Laura, you are both children. It is flattering to have a nice boy notice you and I know that has been a concern of yours, but as they say, easy does it."

"I know Mama, but it is so exciting."

Ida Mae kissed Laura's forehead. "I'm sure it is. A first crush always is. And see, it was not long ago that you thought no boy would ever give you a second glance. Now you see that you have nothing to fear on that account."

"I'm glad he's coming to school here. I can see him every day, but I think that for now, we'll just be good friends."

"That's my girl," Ida Mae said, looking around the kitchen. "I'd better get busy with supper for the men. Laura, will you peel the potatoes for me?"

"Sure Mama."

"After supper, let's work on a notice about our school for the paper."

The demand for educational services for the children of Deadwood exceeded Ida Mae's expectations. Within two weeks she had 23 children attending her classroom in which she taught the fundamentals of reading, writing, and arithmetic for classes one through six. Under her tutelage, students came and went based on their needs and their ability to learn. Ida Mae Stewart saw the "Stewart School," as she called it, her contribution to Deadwood's young regardless of race or ability to pay tuition – a contribution she continued without subsidy even after the public school system was instituted in the community.

"All right, let's be seated," Hiram Custis said. He stood in the doorway to his office and ushered Ryker and Esmeralda Krump inside. "Bella Sue, get out of here!" he kicked at the calico cat, which scooted between his legs towards the lobby. "Prudence, put that blasted cat upstairs where she belongs."

Once seated, Hiram assumed his position behind his desk and folded his hands on the tabletop. Prudence Custis entered and sat near him with a pencil and tablet in her hand. "Today we are meeting for an arbitration conference. Present are…" he motioned to Ryker, "Mister Tobias aka Toby Ryker, of late of the town of Deadwood, and over here, Esmeralda Krump. Also present is Prudence Custis who shall record, verbatim, the content of this conference. The subject of this conference is a delicate one." He paused as Ryker looked out the window and Esmeralda took out a handkerchief. "It concerns the revenge or retribution shooting of the late Mister William Krump by Mister Ryker." He looked at Ryker. "Mister Ryker, please begin."

Switching his gaze from the window, Ryker fixed it on Esmeralda Krump for the first time. It was a cold, angry stare tinged with pain. "Back in the Indian nations in what is now Oklahoma Territory in eighteen hundred and sixty-nine, Willy Krump and his gang were buffalo hunters. I was living in a Pawnee Camp and was married to a wonderful Pawnee Princess named Wild Flower in our lingo. We had a daughter named Hope. At that time, Hope was just over four years old. It was the happiest time of my whole life." The old man's lip began to tremble and tears began to flow down his face. He looked away and Hiram offered him a fresh handkerchief. After he composed himself, he continued.

"Anyway, one day Willy Krump and the others were mad because their take of hides wasn't as big as they thought it should be so they rode into camp looking for more. They were drunk, and as the braves and I were out hunting deer, there were no men of fighting age in camp. So they ransacked it. Tore it to pieces. Worked themselves into a frenzy and started raping and killing, and when they got to our tipi…" again

Ryker broke down, sobbing bitterly. He noticed that Esmeralda was sobbing also. No one spoke until he was able to go on.

"When they got to our tipi, they raped and killed my wife and butchered my little girl. We heard them shooting from the surrounding forests and come a-runnin' but by that time the worst was done. We chased them and killed them all except for your husband, who had a fast horse and got away." Ryker's face turned bitter again. "But I never forgot his face. Nosireebob. It was burned into my brain. I never saw him again until two years back when I was here in Deadwood trading in some gold dust I'd taken from my Potato Creek Mine up yonder in the hills. Willy Krump waited on me! He was dressed up in a suit, but I knew the polecat was him. And what he done all come back to me. So I waited until the bank closed and hid in some brush and when he came along, I shot him for a fact, but not in the vitals. I intended to kill him later for what he did to my family and would have too, but then this dear young girl came out and begged me not to hurt her daddy no more." He looked from Esmeralda to Hiram Custis.

"What could I do? I wanted to kill him so bad on account of what he done, but when I saw that little girl pleading, I also saw my daughter Hope the way she must have begged for mercy so many years ago in that Pawnee camp. So I left him there and I told that girl her daddy would be all right and that I wouldn't hurt him no more. And then I holstered my gun and left. Even went into the Number Ten and told them where Krump lay and to get Doc Peirce or somebody because he needed tending to. Then I rode out. I found out later that the bank posted a reward for me dead or alive because Krump died anyway. A bounty hunter named John McQuiston tracked me clear down to Laramie where I was living with the Stewart family, who now have moved to Deadwood with me. That's a whole different story. Anyway, we shot and killed McQuiston before he had the chance to do the same to me."

Ryker paused. "Don't ask me to feel sorry I shot your husband Mrs. Krump, because I can't. But I do feel bad for what happened because I understand you are on hard times. It ain't your fault what Willy did. Now the law is still saying I am a criminal. Says I assaulted Willy. But from my side of the fence, I gave Willy no more than what he had coming to him, for my wife and daughter deserved to be avenged."

There was silence in the room. After several seconds, Hiram stood up. "Let's take a five minute break, shall we? These are pretty tense issues."

CHAPTER ELEVEN

"All right, let's return to the conference," Custice said after everyone had a chance to stretch their legs. Five minutes had turned into twenty, for the attorney had smoked a cigar as well, but since the time was on Ryker's dime, he figured what the heck. When everyone was again seated and Prudence in her place to take shorthand, he said, "By the way Esmeralda, I thought Camille was coming today."

"That was my intention," Esmeralda said. "But after reconsidering, I thought the better of it. She was barely three years old when this happened and is only five now. I don't want to upset the poor child any further. Besides, there are things that need to be said that she doesn't know, and that she wouldn't understand."

"I see," Hiram said. "It is probably for the best then."

"That young, let her enjoy what is left of her childhood," Ryker agreed.

Esmeralda sighed, turning her beautiful large brown eyes on Ryker. "What you said about William Krump did not come as a shock to me, Mister Ryker. You may think that it did but it didn't. I knew he had a horrible past. He told me some of it, not in detail, but I knew he had killed innocents among the Pawnee Indians. I can tell you this though. He suffered for it. He feared for his life and for ours. He worried that the day would come when you would show up and do what you did, not only to him but also to us. He even tried to track you down after

111

that slaughter and somehow make things right, so he told me, but by that time the tribe had disbanded and you were long gone."

"That's true," Ryker said. "I had no reason to stay around after that."

"He felt bad, felt guilt over those deaths, Mister Ryker. Oftentimes he had night terrors and would wake up crying. But William was not the leader of those buffalo hunters as you think he was. He was just a follower and a weak man like most of the others. He was as much afraid for himself from a man he called Big Jake, who was actually the leader of the hide cutters. Jake led that charge into the camp and told his men he'd carve up anyone who didn't come with him. And William, he believed him. He saw Jake do it many times. He would get drunk and kill his own men for sport."

"There was one we caught named Jake," Toby recalled. "He was a brutal one. We made sure he couldn't hurt anybody no more. Took his eyes and his ears so in the next world, he couldn't see or hear anyone else to harm."

Esmeralda shuddered. "Savage men live savage lives and die savage deaths. Well, William joined another hide cutter crew for a time but he broke away from that bunch a year or so later and drifted for many years. He was mostly a ranch hand. Then, still as a ranch laborer for hire, he wandered up this way, but the lumbago was starting to get to him so he had trouble sitting a horse all day. He drifted into town and started working odd jobs, mostly swamping out the saloons. While he was doing that he met up with J. H. Singleton, the president of the People's Bank. Singleton liked to gamble a bit and he took a shine to William. He hired him on as a janitor at the bank. I was pregnant with Camille at that time and that's when I met him."

"Camille…you mean?"

"That's right. Camille wasn't his by blood. Her father and my husband was a Spaniard named Philippe Santiago Lopez who died of the smallpox before Camille was born. We were heading west when it happened and Deadwood was as far as we got. Philippe is buried in the pauper's section at Mount Moriah. I stayed on here and met William, and he was kind enough to marry me and provide for me even though he knew I was carrying another man's child."

"Well, if that don't beat all," Ryker said. "Did you love Willy Krump?"

"I cannot honestly say that I did, but he was kind and generous to us and when Camille was born, she never knew she wasn't William's daughter. She still doesn't know."

"But he was dressed up and waited on me in the bank."

"William might have been a weak man but he wasn't stupid. He had a quick mind, was good with figures, and often filled in as a teller."

"A teller? McQuiston told me he was an officer of that bank."

"He was no officer. He was a janitor and a part time teller. But J. H. felt a loyalty towards him and when he was shot and then died a few weeks later, he went off half-cocked and issued that reward." Esmeralda looked hard at Ryker. "William had a cancer. He was going blind even before you shot him and knew he was dying. The cancer is what killed him, not your bullet."

"A cancer?" Ryker repeated.

"Yes. Anyway, I tried to talk to Mister Singleton and explain this to him, but emotions were running so high around here, and me just being a woman and everything and a Spanish one at that, no one would listen to me. I finally talked to Judge Mason about it and he ordered an inquest. When Doctor Flora Stanford did the autopsy on William, she saw that your bullet was not intended to kill, Mister Ryker."

Hiram motioned to Prudence. "This is off the record. It just goes to show that things often are not what they first appear to be, Mister Ryker. Even I got caught up in the furor and was influenced by Singleton. As prosecutor for the Territory, I at first believed you should be charged with murder and if captured, you should be hung. After the inquest findings however, I amended the charge against you to assault. After all, you did shoot the man."

"Never denied that," Ryker said.

"We are now on the record," Hiram said to Prudence, who picked up her pencil. "Missus Krump, would you object to the dismissal of the charges of assault against Mister Ryker for his shooting of your late husband William Krump?"

"No, I would not," Esmeralda said. "Had I been in his shoes, knowing what he knew and seeing what he saw, I would have shot William myself. I admire the fact that out of respect for my daughter you did not kill William, Mister Ryker. That would have disturbed her for life."

"Thank you ma'am," Ryker said humbly. "That is a load off my mind. But tell me, how are you and Camille gettin' along, if I may be so bold as to ask?"

"Not well," Esmeralda said. "William owned our cottage free and clear and he had some savings and the bank provided a small insurance policy. But it is about gone."

"Fate has not been kind to you, Missus Krump," Ryker said. "You are a fine lady and through no fault of your own have been dealt several rotten hands. I on the other hand, by the luck of the draw, have been granted more than I am entitled to. Maybe there is some way we can balance things out a bit." He looked at Hiram. "Mister Custis, I intend to place the sum of thirty five hundred dollars into an account for Mrs. Krump and her daughter. That ought to care for them for many years to come."

"That is very generous," Hiram said. "At today's standards with interest, that is an adequate allowance for over ten years. Enough to see Camille to womanhood."

Esmeralda gasped. "Mister Ryker! This certainly is not necessary."

"Not necessary but deserved and I want you to have it. I contributed to taking away your breadwinner and the way I see it, it is only fittin' that I help fill in the gap."

"Our needs are simple," Esmeralda said. "Thank you Mister Ryker, from the bottom of my heart. I shall never forget you."

"Nor I you," Ryker said.

"I think we can close this conference," Hiram said. "Mister Ryker, I have the authority to dismiss the assault case against you and based upon Esmeralda's statements here, that is what I intend to do. I will file the papers at the courthouse tomorrow."

"Wonderful," Ryker said. "This is a great weight off my mind, no ands ifs or buts about it, yesireebob. Missus Krump, the money will be set up in an account in your name at the People's Bank tomorrow."

"*Gracias,*" Esmeralda said, arising to leave. "Thank you."

"Custice, there's a couple more things I want you to do for me," Ryker said as Esmeralda left the office.

After concluding his business with the attorney, Ryker stepped outside and drew a deep breath, glancing around at the sun-filled day and the hills surrounding the city of Deadwood. For the first time in over a year he felt free from the cloud of shame of being a wanted man. He also felt that the deaths of Wild Flower and Hope were vindicated, that they could rest easy now knowing that he had done all in his power to bring their killers to justice, yet grant mercy to the dependants who should not have to suffer for the sins of the father. He imagined the faces of his wife and child outlined in the jagged rock along the creek and heard them sing their approval of his actions in the whistling of the wind through the pines. Smiling, he headed toward the Stewart mansion.

The next day he completed the transaction at the bank as he promised to do and delivered a receipt of the deposit to Hiram Custis's office. Hiram handed him another official looking document. "Here's that other matter you requested.'

Ryker took the document and squinted at it. "Looks nice. What do I owe you?"

"Seventy-three dollars and eighty-five cents including filing fees," Hiram said. "I also updated your will and filed it like you said. Here's a copy."

"Here's payment in gold and well worth it," Ryker said, handing over the money and taking the will. "I hope all goes well for the widow Krump and her daughter."

"Why don't you take the receipt over to her cottage yourself?" Hiram said. "She lives just off the lower end of Main Street."

"Maybe I will. How will I know the place?"

"That's easy," Hiram said. "It's the first street west between the saloons and Chinatown. They are the corner house. She has a statue of the Virgin Mary in her yard."

"The virgin Mary?"

"Yes. Esmeralda is a devout Catholic. They believe in that kind of thing."

"Oh okay, I'll mosey on down then," Ryker said.

About ten minutes later, Ryker found the house Hiram described and approached the front door. He knocked then pressed his face to the window, trying to peer in. "Missus Krump?" He knocked again. "Missus Krump? Are you to home? It's me, Toby Ryker."

Esmeralda Krump appeared from a back room and opened the door. "Good morning, Mister Ryker. Please do come in."

"I seen your Mary virgin out front," Ryker said after entering and taking a seat. "Mister Custis said it was by your house."

"The Virgin Mary, you mean," Esmeralda said. "It is part of our Catholic faith. We believe that Mary is the mother of the Christ child."

"Well, somebody had to be his mother, I reckon," Ryker said. "But I don't know how she could be no virgin then."

"Because she did not know man."

"How can that be?"

"I'd be most happy to explain my religion to you, Mister Ryker," Esmeralda said.

"I went to a Catholic church once out in Colorady. It was one of them there Mission churches and I didn't have anything better to do that day. The minister, he –"

"Priest."

"Huh?"

"We call our ministers priests."

"Oh, I see. Well anyway, this ah, priest, he was dressed in kind of a holy dress and he kept saying 'Dominic's biscuits,' and two boys up there with him, they was wearing dresses too and they kept bobbing up and down and striking their chests and ringing bells and saying things like 'And come spear it two to old.' So when I heard them talkin' thataway, well, it didn't make a lick of sense to me so I up and left."

By this time, Esmeralda was nearly hysterical with laughter. "Mister Ryker, I haven't been this amused in a long time. Thank you. It is good to laugh."

"Yes, it is," Ryker said, grinning. "People don't stop and do enough of that nowadays."

"What you were hearing was Latin," Esmeralda explained. "Our religious services are in Latin. It is very similar to Spanish, which is one reason why the Catholic faith is so dear to me."

"Latin, yeah that's what it was," Ryker said.

That priest was saying, 'Dominus vobiscum,' which is a Latin greeting meaning, 'The Lord be with you.' And those alter boys as we call them, they were saying, 'Et cum spiritu tuo' which means, 'And with your spirit.' So, when you put the two greetings together, you have..." she leaned her hands and tilted her head to the left, "Dominus Vobiscum, The Lord be with you..."she leaned her hands and tilted her head to the right, "Et cum spiritu tuo, And with your spirit."

"Well now ain't that peachy," Ryker said. "When you say it like that, it makes sense."

"We have prayer books nowdays that translate the Latin into English," Esmeralda said. "Maybe you would like to come out to our church this Sunday."

"Nope," Ryker said quickly as he shook his head and waved her away. "No offense Missus Krump, but I been stomping around this here earth the better part of seventy years now without being a churchgoer and I reckon it's a little late for me to change my ways. I have my Almighty, don't get me wrong, but he lives out yonder in the hills and forests, not in a church."

"As you wish, Mister Ryker."

"Please call me Toby."

"I will. And I would be honored if you were to call me Esmeralda."

"Esmeralda it is. And the reason I came out is I wanted to give you this receipt from the bank. It shows that the money we talked about is deposited in your name at the People's Bank." As Ryker spoke, a young girl appeared from the back room and Esmeralda spoke to her in Spanish.

"I bet this charmer is Camille." The girl stared at Ryker silently. "She probably doesn't remember me." Then he frowned. "Of course, the only time she saw me was…"

Esmeralda spoke to Camille some more and motioned to Ryker. The girl came over to him then and hugged him and said *Abuelo* and sat on his knee. Ryker kissed her and looked at Esmeralda questioningly.

"I told her you were her grandfather. It is a title we use not only for our blood grandfathers but also for elderly men whom we revere."

Ryker smiled at Camille and hugged her once more. Camille then crawled from his lap and disappeared into the back room again.

"And no, she does not remember you from that incident," Esmeralda said. "I will never tell her. She does not need to know."

"Thank you for that. What will you do now?"

"Because of your generosity, I can take my time," Esmeralda said. "However, there is a fine gentleman, a widower I met at our church whom has shown some interest in me. He is Juan Carlos Lopez and he runs the Mexican restaurant on Main Street. He makes the best tortilla in town."

"A widower, huh?"

"Yes, his wife died in a prairie fire that took their home a few years back. Very sad. He was left with five children."

"So being a Catholic may be about more than religion for you, eh, Esmeralda?"

Esmeralda smiled. "Maybe. Who knows? I might be Esmeralda Lopez once again."

After bidding Esmeralda and Camille goodbye, Ryker headed back toward the Stewart mansion. On the way he happened by an office that had two shingles out front saying "Dr. Flora Hayward Stanford M.D." and "Doctor Norman Taggart M.D." He entered.

"Doctor Stanford? My name is Toby Ryker. I live with the David Stewart family."

A well-groomed woman wearing a white doctor's gown with a stethoscope wrapped around her neck extended her hand. "Mister Ryker. I have heard of you."

"Oh? From who?"

"Poker Alice. She is a patient of mine."

"Well I declare. It's a pretty small world, I guess. I ain't ever met a lady doctor before."

"A lot of men don't put much faith in our ability," Doctor Stanford said. "I assure you that I am a duly licensed physician. Besides this office, I have a second practice in Sundance Wyoming."

"I'm sure you are fully qualified," Ryker said. "And no disrespect was meant when I said you were a woman and all. In my years, I've learned that women can do things just as well as men and some things a heck of a lot better."

"That is refreshing to hear. How may I help you?"

"Well, one of your fellow doctors down Wyoming way, Doc Swensen in Laramie, he says I got a bad ticker. Heart failure was what he called it. He gave me some pills."

"I know Magnus Swensen. He and Doctor McGillycuddy are acquainted also. He's a cantankerous old character, isn't he?"

"That he is. I guess that's why he and I got along famously."

"Have you been having problems?" the doctor asked.

"Kind of," Ryker said. "I go walking every day as part of my treatment and I'm on a strict diet. Don't eat much meat. Lost a hundred pounds now, but I notice of late I get short of breath easy and I get tired."

Doctor Stanford patted the examining table. "Sit up here." After doing as requested, the physician put her stethoscope to her ears and listened carefully to Ryker's his chest and back in several places. After two or three minutes she removed the scope and said, "Yes, you have congestive heart failure. But then, you already know that. I can hear your heart valves clicking mid-systolic. They are not supposed to click."

"Does that mean I've bought the farm?" Ryker asked.

"Not necessarily. How old are you, Mister Ryker?"

"Just about seventy."

"That is well past the average life expectancy. I bury many of my patients much younger than seventy. What sort of pills does Dr. Swensen have you on?"

"He calls them nitros."

"Nitroglycerin, a standard treatment. Do you take them?"

"Didn't have to for a long time but lately I've been taking them again."

"Bring in the bottle, will you please? I'm here Tuesdays, Thursdays, and Saturday mornings. I want to check your dosage. We may have to increase it."

"Doc," Ryker said quietly, "What am I looking at here? What can I expect?"

Doctor Stanford took a deep breath and squinted at the old man. "Mister Ryker, as Doctor Swensen undoubtedly told you, congestive heart failure is a degenerative condition. It never gets better. It just gets worse. You seem to be doing all the right things and I commend you for that. But your heart is a pump. Its job is to pump blood, but with congestive heart failure it gets weaker and as it weakens it is less able to circulate blood through your body. As that happens you get short of breath and you get tired." She walked over to the cistern pump resting on the dry sink. "Come here." Ryker ambled over and the doctor primed the pump and began to pump it full and deep. "See how the water rushes out?"

"Yeah."

"That is like a healthy heart working at full capacity. Now watch this." She slowed down her strokes to half. The water also slowed. "See what's happening?"

"Uh-huh."

"As the heart weakens, it does not pump as fully. Then the blood does not circulate as well until..." she further slowed the stroke until just a trickle came out, "it reaches the point where the pump is not circulating an adequate supply of blood."

"So one day it will stop pumping then?"

"Yes, one day it will stop pumping." She banged the handle against the base and the water ceased. "You lose consciousness and you die." She smiled. "All in all, it is not an unpleasant way to die."

"When will it happen?"

"I have no way of knowing. It is just one of those things that when it happens, it happens. It could be a week, it could be a year, or it could be ten years. No one knows. The good thing about nitroglycerin is that it eases chest pain, or angina as we call it, so the process is relatively comfortable for you. I suggest you keep doing what you are doing, Mister Ryker."

"Okay Doc, thanks. I'll bring that pill bottle in. What do I owe you?"

"Nothing now. We'll settle up when I fill the prescription. It will come to eight dollars."

Ryker withdrew the money. "I'll be back on Thursday. Here ya go. Paid in advance."

"That's something I don't see very often," Doctor Stanford said, chuckling.

"See you Thursday," Ryker said, heading out the door. He paused and looked back, "Unless my ticker decides to quit on me before then."

As Ida Mae's school classes were still in session, Ryker took the opportunity to get in his walk for the day. He returned in time for the supper meal and after supper he said, "That attorney Custis is a good feller. He got the charges again' me dropped and I settled accounts with the widow of Willy Krump so that she and her daughter won't have to go wanting."

"That's wonderful, Toby," Ida Mae said.

"I bet that's a load off your mind," David added.

"That it is," Ryker said. "And there's more. He pulled out the document he had received from Custice. "Now I'm a legal member of the family." He grinned, passing the document to David. "See what it says there?"

David looked at the paper, smiled, and passed it on to Ida Mae. "You went ahead and did it, didn't you?"

"Sure did. I am now Toby Ryker Stewart, all legal like. Had my name changed by Mister Custis. He filed it at the courthouse and everything."

"This is an honor, Toby," Ida Mae said.

"Yes, Grandpa Ryker, I mean, Grandpa Stewart," Laura said.

"Yeah, Grandpa," Pauly said, hugging him.

"Since I ain't got a family of my own, there's no family I'd rather be a part of than this one," Ryker said, getting tears in his eyes. "You make an old man proud."

David looked hard at Ryker. "Toby, getting the charges dismissed, settling with the widow, buying the house for Matthew and Becky, willing us the mine...are you fixing to do something?"

"Matthew asked me that a while back too," Ryker said. "Just getting things in order David, just getting things in order, that's all. If I learned one thing over all these years, it's that you need to be prepared because you never know what is going to happen next. On the way home today I stopped in to see that lady doctor in town, Flora Stanford. She wants to see my medicine, Sarge. Maybe adjust the dosage or something." He looked at the children then back at David and Ida Mae and chose his words carefully. "My last great adventure may not be that far off."

CHAPTER TWELVE

The next several months, which took the Stewarts into the Christmas holiday season of 1887, could not have been better. The Potato Creek Mine produced ever greater yields of gold ore and the veins, which followed the contours of the quartz bedrock and descended into the earth, grew wider. There were weeks when the mine produced a thousand dollars in gold with no end in sight.

Becky's pregnancy proceeded into the second trimester and all was well. She began to show and felt wonderful. Matthew and she grew closer as they anticipated the birth of their first child.

Ida Mae's "Stewart School" flourished. Under her tutelage the young and the disenfranchised of Deadwood received the basic education necessary to give them a fighting chance in the competitive world about them. Some learned quickly, and like Becky, departed after but a few months; others lingered far longer. Toby Ryker financed it all, purchasing supplies as needed and ordering primer books from the Henry Holt Company.

As with his prediction that the Wyoming ranch would sell, Ryker's comment that night at the supper table that "you never know what's going to happen next" also proved prophetic. Just when things couldn't get any better, turmoil struck.

Gene Lattimore stumbled up to the Potato Creek Mine holding his hand to his bloody shoulder. "I'm sorry Mister Stewart. I'm afraid they got your gold."

"Gene," David said, running from the office. "What happened to you?"

"They were waiting in ambush about a half mile down. I need to hire a guard, I guess."

"How'd they know?"

"How do they ever know?" Gene said. "Word trickles out from everywhere when gold production picks up. There's plenty out there that would rather take it than work for it."

"Did you recognize any of them?"

"There were four of them that rushed me. Fired one shot that grazed me, grabbed the strongbox, and headed toward Spearfish Canyon. The one they called Otto rode a Missouri mule. He had a long beard. All of them looked like hill folk."

"Robbers like that shouldn't be too hard to find," David said. "Let's get you back town and have that shoulder tended to. I'll report this to Seth. Matthew! Come here!"

Within the hour, David, Matthew, and Gene were in Deadwood. They took Gene to Doc Taggert's office where he was tended to then hastened to Seth Bullock's office.

"Seth, we've been robbed," David said.

"They shot Gene Lattimore," Matthew added. "He's over at Doc Taggert's."

"Do you know who?" Seth said, reaching for his guns.

"Gene said there were four of them. One was called Otto, and he rode a mule," David said. "They took the strongbox and high-tailed it toward Spearfish Canyon."

"Otto Cobb and his boys," Seth said, nodding his head. "Lazy, worthless trash from the hill country down south. Moonshiners, but besides being a drunk, Otto is a few bricks shy of a load. He's tried stunts like this before although this is the first time he's ever shot anyone. They have a shack in Spearfish Canyon. Been squatting there better than a year now." He pulled two badges out of his desk. "I could use your help."

"Sure Seth, we'll come," David said.

"Yeah, I'm in too," Matthew replied as father and son pinned on the badges.

"Figured I could count on you both. Raise your right hands." When David and Matthew had done so, Seth said, "Will you uphold the laws of the United States and this Territory to the best of your ability?" Both David and Matthew agreed they would. "Good, you're deputized. Now let's ride."

David and Seth stopped to tell Ida Mae what they were up to while Matthew rode home and told Becky the same. Becky felt herself tense up as she watched Matthew strap on his revolver and grab his 30 caliber Winchester rifle out of the cabinet. "Do be careful, Mattie," she said, a term of endearment she used to refer to him in their private moments.

"Don't worry," Matthew said. "I'll be fine. Those idiots are no match for Pa and Seth and me. I won't let them steal our gold." When he saw how nervous she was, he said, "Why don't you go over and stay with Ma and Grandpa Toby while we're gone? This will probably all be over in a couple hours."

"Okay Mattie, I will." She kissed him. "Hurry back." She gazed out the window while her handsome young husband, now badged and turned lawman, slid the Winchester into the scabbard, mounted Wino, and galloped away.

The posse of three headed toward Spearfish Canyon hoping to overtake Otto Cobb and his boys before they holed up in their shack, but it was not meant to be. It was a three hour ride from Deadwood to the shack, which put the men at the perimeter shortly after two o'clock. The Cobbs were already there as evidenced by their horses and the mule tied out front.

"Doggone it Rudy, gimme that," Hezeckiel "Pig Eye" Cobb said as he tried to wrestle the gallon shoulder jug from his youngest brother.

"Go fetch your own!" Rudy said. "There's ten more jugs just like this one sittin' by the still. Pa, tell this dumb ox to quit!"

Otto Cobb, the patriarch of the family, was in poor health. He now sat next to the table containing the strongbox with a whiskey jug in his lap. Years of drinking shine left him with a bad liver. His abdomen was bloated and the whites of his eyes had a yellow tint to them. He tended to drift in and out of reality and to hallucinate, and at the moment he was combing the fingers of his left hand through his beard and studying the wall intently. Rudy's request went unheard. "What's them cotton-mouths doin' a-crawlin' up the wall yonder?"

Zebulon "Rooster" Cobb, the eldest of the three Cobb boys, slouched in a chair with the back broken off that was precariously tipped back on the hind legs against the dry sink. A half empty whiskey jug also rested in his lap. "Them ain't cottonmouths Pa, them's water moccasins. Don't you know your snakes?" He giggled and looked at his brothers who giggled back.

"Pa's brain is cookin' today," said Pig Eye.

"Yeah, what brain he has left that hasn't already cooked down to pudding," Rudy said.

Rooster was taking a gulp from the jug as Rudy spoke and began laughing. Leaning back further, the chair slid out from under him and he fell to the floor.

"Lookee that cottonmouth there," Otto said. "He's wearing a hat!" How can he do that? He ain't got no ears. You see that too, don't you, Ma?" When he heard Rooster crash to the floor he hollered, "Come on in! The door's open!"

"Wipe yer boots off first," Rooster yelled, still sitting on the floor and laughing hysterically. "We Cobbs keep a tidy house!"

"You pushed Ma down the well and she drownded. Ma's gone. How many times we got to tell you that, Pa?" Rudy said.

"Oh no, that ain't true," Otto said."I see her most everynight lookin' down from the rafters."

"Otto Cobb!" hollered Seth from the safety of the boulders sur-rounding the shack.

"Wh-who said that?" Otto replied, glancing around. "You say that, Rudy?"

Pig Eye wandered over to the window and caught sight of move-ment outside. "What in tarnation is going on out there?" He pointed the barrel of his rifle through the paneless window. "Somethin's movin' around out there."

Rudy looked too. "That's your horse, you pea brain."

Pig Eye squinted. "Oh yeah, so it is. As blurry as my eyes are a-gettin' I thought I was seein' a squirrel in that tree yonder."

"That'd have to be a darn big squirrel," Rudy replied. "And that tree you think you're pointin' at is a rock. It ain't even green like a tree, for cripes sake."

"Otto Cobb!" Seth hollered again. This time he fired a round above the roof. "This is Marshal Seth Bullock and a posse of more men than you can count. We know you are in there and we know you held up the Lattimore Dray Line this morning. You and your boys have exactly two minutes to come out with your hands up!"

There was a commotion inside the shack and it sounded like someone tripped over a pail.

"We ain't coming out, lawman!" someone shouted.

"Yeah, we didn't steal no strongbox," another voice yelled. "Quit pickin' on us Cobbs!"

Seth raised his eyebrows at David and Matthew and adjusted his hat. "Morons, the lot of them. Dumber than sheep." The three men saw a rifle barrel poke through a window and saw a puff of smoke followed a split second later by a gunshot and the sound of a bullet as it ricocheted off the rock above them.

Matthew returned fire through the window with his Winchester. The men heard the sound of glass breaking and much cussing and swearing from inside.

"Them dang snakes are shootin' at us!" Otto screamed. "Where's my pistol when I need it? Who stole my gun, dagnabbit!"

"It's hangin' in your holster Pa," Rudy said.

"Oh here it is! Never mind, it was a-hangin' in my holster by my leg here. Pig Eye, take your rifle and give them snakes what for again while I reload."

Pig Eye stuck his rifle out the window again, turned his head, gritted his teeth and closed his eyes as he pulled the trigger, narrowly missing their horses. The bullet whizzed toward the three lawmen and ricocheted closer to their heads this time.

"They're just smart enough to be dangerous," David said.

"I'll bet next month's wages they're drunk already," Seth said, looking around. "It appears to me they have a fire burning in there. See the smoke coming out of that stack?"

"I see it," David said.

"If we could plug that stack, we could smoke them out," Seth said.

"I can sneak up and do that," Matthew said. "There's a trail off to the left here that runs close to the side of the shack. It has pretty good cover too." He pointed. "See where that mound is there? If you can keep them occupied, I can get onto the roof from there."

"Be careful," Seth said.

"And be quiet," David said. "If they hear you on the roof, they'll shoot right through it."

"I will Pa. Maybe when you see me begin to climb up there, you can start shooting and keep them distracted."

"Good idea," Seth said, picking up a flat rock. "Cover the stovepipe with this."

"Okay." Matthew grabbed the rock and stole around and got into position then looked back at David and Seth and nodded.

Back in Deadwood, Ida Mae dismissed classes early. She did not tell Laura or Pauly of the matter at hand, but told them to go out and enjoy the day. Laura saddled and bridled the fancy brown and white Welsh pony that David just bought her, which she named Stormy, and rode off toward one of her favorite trails along the creek. Pauly and Chen disappeared to heaven knows where. This left Ryker and the two Stewart women alone in the mansion where they paced, each fretting about David and Matthew.

"These things are so dang unpredictable Sarge," Ryker said.

"I hope it doesn't come to a shootout," Becky said.

"Maybe they will just surrender," Ida Mae said.

The pacing continued, the only sound that of the mantle clock ticking.

"We can always hope so," Ryker said. "But my guts just don't feel good about this."

"Time's about up Cobb," Seth shouted.

"Wait! Wait!" There was more noise inside the shack.

Matthew looked to Seth and shrugged his shoulders but did not climb onto the roof. Since the shack was a partial dugout on his side, he was standing nearly at roof level anyway. He felt his heart beginning to race.

"Okay lawman, we're coming out," a voice yelled. "Don't shoot!" The door opened and Otto Cobb and two of his boys stepped outside. They dropped their rifles and stood, legs spread. "Here we are," Otto said.

"Where's the other one?" Seth demanded.

"Rudy ain't here," Otto said. "He's, ah –"

He's at an auction sale," Pig Eye said, nodding at Rooster.

"Yeah, that's right, he went to an auction sale to get us some new curtains," Rooster added, grinning back at Pig Eye.

"Step out from behind them rocks so we can surrender to you all," Otto said.

Matthew saw a shadow and glanced around. A figure was moving toward him from around the back side of the shack. He realized there obviously was a rear getaway door and this was obviously Rudy. The Cobbs were trying to bushwhack Seth and David. As Matthew drew back the hammer on his Winchester, Rudy looked up.

"What the –" Rudy drew his revolver and aimed it at Matthew's head. Matthew fired the Winchester. His heart thumping wildly now, the adrenalin coursing through him, Matthew levered another shell into the chamber as Rudy Cobb tumbled backward and fell into a heap on the ground.

At the sound of the rifle, Otto screamed, "There's another snake behind us and this one's totin' a Winchester!" He pulled his revolver and fired straight up into the air rather than toward Seth and David, who had moved out from the rocks.

Pig Eye and Rooster also pulled their guns and put their backs against one another, one firing toward David, narrowly missing him, and one firing toward Matthew. David shouldered his Winchester, took careful aim, and caught Pig Eye in the forehead, knocking him over.

Crawling to his knees, Rudy cocked his revolver and was about to raise it when Matthew's Winchester roared again. This time when Rudy fell down, he did not move. Rising up cautiously, Matthew felt a sharp pain in his leg and fell over.

"I got him, Pa!" Rooster said, his yellow teeth grinning at Otto, seeking his approval. Otto nodded at him and smiled back. At least, Rooster was destined die a contented man. Seth and David both fired at Rooster, dropping him in his tracks with heart-lung shots.

The only Cobb still standing was Otto who now looked around him, bewildered. He had fired only one shot, the one he fired straight up into the air at nothing. "My boys," he said.

Turning away from David and Seth, Otto knelt beside Pig Eye and Rooster who lay next to each other in death. "Piggie…Roo-Rooster," he whispered, and then he started to rave. "And where's my Rudy!" Otto stood up and stumbled, gun in hand, toward the shack while Seth and David moved slowly toward him. They were concerned for Matthew, who was not moving, and did not know if the old man saw him or not.

"Stop right there, Cobb! It's over," Seth said, raising his Peacemaker and aiming it at Otto's back. "Turn around and drop the gun."

Otto, now trembling, turned his anguished face to his tormenters. "You snakes killed my boys!" he bawled. "I can't go on without my boys!" With that, Otto Cobb began to raise the revolver.

"Cobb, drop it right there!" Seth said, cocking his Colt.

Unhearing, Otto re-cocked and continued to raise the revolver. He glanced at the bodies of his sons again. "My boys," he whispered. "I'm a-comin' boys. Wait for me 'n we'll all visit your maw together." He nodded at the bodies with an eerie smile. "Boy, will she ever be surprised." With a shaky hand, he raised the pistol to his head, stuck the barrel into his mouth and pulled the trigger.

David ran to Matthew while Seth checked Otto Cobb and the three boys, collected their weapons, and assured himself that their robbing days were over. When the marshal checked inside the shack, he saw the Lattimore Dray Line strongbox, still unopened, sitting on an old table in the center of the room.

"It hurts like blazes, Pa," Matthew said.

"Yes, the one they called Rooster hit you in the calf," David said. "It doesn't look like he broke the bone, but we need to get you to a doctor right away. I hope we can save your leg."

"Oh Pa, my leg!"

"Infection is the problem," David said. "You won't be walking on it now. We'll make a travois to get you back to Deadwood like we did for Toby when we brought him down from the Medicine Bow Mountains. That's the safest way to get you to town."

Seth and David rigged a travois from a bedroll out of the shack that they rigged between two poles and attached to Wino, who was used to toting this sort of thing. After resting Matthew gently upon it, they put the strongbox there too. They slung the bodies of the Cobb men over their mounts, and the macabre procession headed back to Deadwood. They went to Doctor Norman Taggert's office first.

"Matthew was injured while on official business," Seth said. "My office will pay his medical costs."

"Sure Seth," Doc replied. "I'll get him cleaned up and we'll see what we have here."

David waited with Matthew while Seth headed over to the funeral parlor. He made arrangements for the bodies to be prepared for burial and an official notice to any next of kin posted.

"It will cost the government more than they were worth just to plant them on Mount Moriah," Seth said.

"No one will claim them," Magellan Fry the undertaker declared, motioning to the four lifeless human forms of the Cobbs. Now in death they bore the final indignity of lying naked in the preparation room on gurneys.

"Just the same, it's the law," Seth said. "And we have to post the notices."

"I'll hose them down, embalm, dress them in new union suits, stick them in pine boxes, and bury them in the paupers section at Mount Moriah," Magellan said. "That's the cheapest way."

"Obliged," Seth said, adjusting his hat.

"Here's another thought. What if I lay them out in the warehouse for a few days after they're prepared," Magellan said. "Folks might pay a quarter to see these idiots before I plant them."

"There's an idea," the marshal replied. "I'll mention it in the newspaper article. Doc Peirce made twenty-eight dollars off those three Indians we hung. Anything you get can be put toward costs. Bill me the rest. I'll see that it's taken care of."

"That I will," Magellan said. "You're my best customer, Seth."

"Ain't proud of it," Bullock replied, heading to the door. "I'd best get over to the newspaper office then check on Matthew Stewart again."

"He is one lucky man," Doc Taggert said to David. "The bullet grazed him, tore up the flesh, and did some tendon damage, but it exited. The bullet isn't in there probably because of the angle of the trajectory."

"Thank the good Lord for that," David said. "He was standing above the shooter who was aiming up at him."

"There you go," the doctor said. "Still, there will be an extensive recovery period. I would like Doctor Stanford to take a look at him too. She is more skilled at this muscle work than I am. She can give him some exercises."

"Will he be able to walk?" David asked.

"Oh sure, sure, but he may have a slight limp and as he gets older, he'll end up with the rheumatism."

David looked down at his son now sleeping peacefully under the influence of the laudanum the doctor gave him. His leg, stitched and bandaged, was swollen. "He'll need crutches, Doc."

"Yes he will, for a time," Doc Taggert said, 'and I have a set which are adjustable to his height. He should rest up a day or two, but I would encourage him to start working that leg as soon as possible. Otherwise he can form blood clots and the muscle can whither."

"It's important we see Doctor Flora right away then."

"Most definitely; you should bring him in tomorrow."

"Hot off the press," Seth said, handing over a copy of the newspaper when David stepped out of the examining room. David glanced at the headline which read: **COBB GANG KILLED** and under that the by-line, *Marshal Seth Bullock Thwarts Mine Robbers.*

"We are darn lucky," David said. "It appears to be a fairly minor wound, but Matthew will be on crutches for a time. Taggert wants Doc Stanford to look at him."

"Good," the marshal said, removing his hat. "What a day."

"It started out fine," David said. "A thousand dollars in gold on the way to the bank and now, four men dead and Matthew and Gene Lattimore wounded. We all would have been better off if we would have stayed in bed today."

The marshal laughed. "What's going to happen will happen sooner or later. I have the strongbox over at the jail."

"You know something? Right now I don't even want to look at that gold, Seth. It caused more than a thousand dollars worth of trouble today."

Doc Taggert stuck his head out from the examining room. "He's awake, Mister Stewart."

"Okay Doc, coming." David addressed the lawman. "Seth, hang onto the gold a few days, will you? I need to get Matthew home."

"Sure," Seth said. "I'll store it in the safe at the jail."

"By the way," Doc Taggert said, "Gene Lattimore patched up okay. His wound wasn't even as deep as Matthews was."

"Lucky for us the Cobbs were lousy shots," David said.

"That's for dang sure," Doc agreed.

David followed by Seth entered the examining room to find Matthew, groggy, looking around. "Hello lawman," David said. "How are you feeling?"

Matthew licked his lips. "Like a stagecoach ran over me. And I got a headache."

David helped his son into a sitting position. "Easy does it."

"You did a fine job out there Matthew," Seth said.

"A fine job of getting shot," Matthew said, wincing.

"Your keen eyesight and sound hearing is what saved you," David said. "Had it been either of us old tomcats, we would have taken Rudy Cobb's bullet and gotten killed."

"Speak for yourself David, "Seth said, laughing. "And who are you calling an old tomcat?"

Matthew found himself chuckling too, in spite of his discomfort. "I'm just glad it's over. Had some crazy dreams while I was sleeping, and who in the dickens is Rudy Cobb?"

"Rudy Cobb is the outlaw you killed," Seth said.

"I did? I killed somebody?"

"Yeah," David replied. "He's the one that snuck up on you from behind."

"He's still feeling the effects of the laudanum," Doc Taggert said. "He'll remember after he comes out of it, but he's going to be mighty sore." The physician rummaged through his pill drawer. "Here, give him two of these pills every four hours. And a shot of whiskey now and then won't hurt him either."

"Anyway Matthew, I'm proud to have you ride with me," the marshal said. "I hope you will do it again."

"Yeah, sure I will."

"A good son you have here David," Seth said, slapping David on the back. "Hope you know that."

"I know it," David said, smiling at Matthew. "Let's get you onto the travois."

David and Seth helped Matthew hobble to the door and lie on the travois that was still attached to Wino. Matthew groaned a couple of times when he bumped his leg. "Let's take him to our house instead of to his," David said. "We can keep a better eye on him, Becky being pregnant and all."

Ten minutes later, Matthew, with the family gathered around him, was resting comfortably on the feinting couch in the front room of the Stewart mansion. Becky knelt by his side and held his hand.

"I remember that Rudy now, dad," Matthew said. "He wasn't much more than a boy. I don't know who was more scared, him or me."

"You did what you had to do," David said. "And if you hadn't shot him, it wouldn't have stopped him from killing you."

"Oh Matthew," Becky said, pressing his hand to her cheek. "Don't ever be a lawman again. Promise me?"

"I don't know that I can do that, Becky. There are times when a man has to help the law and protect what is his. It is part of being a good citizen." Matthew kissed her. "I'll try and be more careful though. This being shot is no fun," he added as the family laughed.

"Seth recovered the gold," David said. "He has it in his safe. And look at the newspaper." He handed it to Matthew.

"It sounds like Marshal Bullock solved this crime single-handed." Matthew laughed as he read the article.

"We are mentioned in there," David said. "But old Seth, he's a politician."

"You know something dad, we should do something special with that gold. That is the hardest thousand dollars we ever earned."

"We could throw a big party up at the mine," David said.

"I could supply the table wine," Ryker said.

"No, I mean something *really* special. How about a trip for all of us."

"Do you mean a vacation?" Ida Mae said.

"Yes, and extended vacation. We'll go west to California, go up the coast into Canada, head east from there," Matthew said. We can turn the mine over to Lei Wong. He and Frankie Malone can run it for a few months while we travel the continent. Now is as good a time as any to go."

"Let's go east first," Ida Mae said, warming to the idea. "We can celebrate Christmas in Maine where I was born."

"That sounds like a wonderful idea," David said, hugging Ida Mae. "Frankly, I told Seth that thousand was more trouble than it was worth. This way, we can all get some good out of it."

The Stewarts proceeded with Matthew's plan and spent the next four months on the tour of a lifetime. It cost them more than the thousand dollars, but considering the returns the Potato Creek Mine was producing, it was a mere pittance. They saw not only villages and cities, but two oceans and crossed several mountains besides the plains and visited ranches, hunters, and tradesmen of all sorts, enjoyed Buffalo Bill's Wild West Show, and bought treasures to return to their homes in Deadwood. Laura celebrated her 12th birthday on tour, and Pauly turned 8. They also spent Christmas in Maine with Ida Mae's relatives and some time in northern Minnesota where Ryker spent his youth. His Ojibwe mother Fawn, at the ripe old age of 83, had joined his father Oliver in the Great Fur Trappers Renvezvous in the Clouds the previous year. Still, the trip home and visiting with her tribe brought back long-forgotten memories to the old mountain man. By the time the entourage returned to Deadwood, Matthew was walking unaided by crutches. He did not even limp, showing only a scar to remind him of his wound, which healed even better than Doctor Stanford hoped, undoubtedly because of his youthful vigor. Life was once again good, at least for the moment.

Deadwood Days

CHAPTER THIRTEEN

"All right, you mangy hombres, slap leather!"

"But, all we want to do is steal this gold, that's all."

"Your stealing days are over. We caught you red-handed. Now slap leather or we'll drop you where you stand."

"Please, Marshal Bullock, you and your men are so fearsome. Can't we work something out? We'll split it with you."

"Trying to bribe officers of the law eh? You're just digging your hole deeper, you no-good, low-down, mangy sidewinders. And besides, it's our gold to begin with, you stupid idiots. Why would we split it with you? Draw!"

The scene of David and Matthew's exploits played out several times during recess this fine spring day at the Stewart school. Pauly "Matthew" Stewart, Chen "Pa David," and Tommy "Seth Bullock" Jones, posed in their gunfighter stances and wearing toy guns and tin stars, stood their ground on one end of the yard. On the other end, the cowardly Cobbs, portrayed by the Dobkins boys, took the same stance, but they didn't have a prayer and they knew it. When the shooting started, they had barely cleared leather before the forces of law and order brought them to an untimely end. They were still writhing in their death throes in the grass while Pauly writhed likewise, holding his leg and crying, "Oh Becky, my darling, I shall crawl to you!"

Ida Mae's school bell clanged. "Children, get up off that ground! You'll end up with grass stains on your clothes. What will your mothers think?" Once decorum had been restored, Ida Mae marched her wards into the classroom and finished the session for that day. After class was dismissed and the students filed out, Pauly motioned to Chen. "Come here."

"What you got?"

"A postcard from my girlfriend in Wyoming, that's what."

The two boys hastened to Pauly's room where he removed the card from his dresser drawer and read it aloud.

Dear Pauly,
How are you? I am fine. I wish the weather was warmer. Is it cold in Deadwood, too? Papa got the gout. I miss you.
Love and kisses, Amanda Buckley.

Pauly showed the card to Chen to prove he wasn't making the words up.

"Gosh, you got a real girlfriend?" Chen said.

"Yup," Pauly said, puffing up his chest proudly.

"Have you ever seen her…you know, naked?"

"No, of course not," Pauly said, suddenly blushing. "Why the heck would I want to?"

"I seen my mom lots of times," Chen said. "And my sister too. "We all sleep in the same room, you know."

"You do?" Pauly said.

"I even seen mom and dad doing it," Chen said.

"Doing what?"

"You know…coupling, like dogs do."

"In front of you?" Pauly said, wrinkling up his nose.

"What's so bad about it?" Chen said. "That's how you and I were made, you know. Your mom and dad do it too."

Pauly stared at Chen, saying nothing.

"Well, they do," Chen said. "What do you think, dumbbell? Do you think some stork dropped you down the chimney?"

After a long pause, Pauly replied, "I guess I never thought about it. Amanda though, she always wanted to play house. Wanted me to be the daddy and her to be the mommy and her doll was supposed to be our daughter. I thought it was stupid."

"Not much fun, huh?"

"No, what's fun about that? Sitting and saying 'Yes dear' and 'Fine, darling' and drinking pretend coffee out of pretend cups. She never wanted to do fun things like pull worms apart or catch garter snakes down by the creek and spin them around by their tails. None of that."

"Or wrestle?"

"Or wrestle," Pauly said, grinning. "Wrestling's the most fun of all, and she'd never do that. Girls really aren't much fun, Chen." He threw the post card on the bed and got Chen in a headlock. The two of them giggled and fell to the floor. "Now *this* is fun!"

"Just like I remember it, David." Ryker glanced around the Potato Creek Mine, nodding approvingly. "Well, not exactly. It's a lot fancier now with the new equipment and all." He had driven the team up to the mine to pay David a visit.

"Toby, glad you came up. Look at these ore samples. This mine you gave us keeps getting richer. Are you sure you don't want it back?"

"Nope," Ryker said. "And besides, I don't need the money and my working days are over. I'm glad I could pass it on to the family." He shielded his eyes from the sun with his hand. "Say, that's Johnny Perrett down there."

"The one they call Potato Creek Johnny?"

"Yeah."

"I wondered who that was. Saw him working the creek below the mine from time to time. Do you want to go down there and visit the midget?"

"Sure, why not?" Ryker said.

"I got an idea," David said. "Come here." He showed Ryker a huge nugget of pure gold that ran fully three ounces. "Found this in the shaft. Let's salt the creek with it where Johnny is sure to find it."

"That will tickle him pink," Ryker said, taking the nugget. "Okay."

Hopping onto the buckboard, Ryker and David rode downstream towards the elfin figure of Potato Creek Johnny. He was panning in the creek and stood waving at them as they waved back.

"Howdy, Tater Creek," Ryker said. "See ya ain't grown none."

"Nope," Johnny said. "In fact I think standing in this cold water has shrunk me a mite. Four-foot-two the last time I checked."

Ryker chuckled as he climbed out of the buckboard and shook hands with Johnny. "Good to see you again, Tater Creek."

"You too," Johnny said. "How long has it been?"

"Two years," Ryker said. "Two years since I was here last. This here is David Stewart. He's taken over the mine for me and old Stumpy."

Johnny held out his hand. "Mister Stewart, glad to meet you. Seen you from a distance."

"Don't make yourself a stranger," David said. "Come on up to the mine any time. The coffee is always on."

"I'll bring some biscuits. I make darn good biscuits even if I do say so myself."

"Tater Creek's right about that David," Ryker said. "I've et some of his biscuits and they're mighty tasty."

"I'll buy some honey then," David said. "Say Johnny, –"

"Johnny."

"Huh?"

"Johnny," Potato Creek Johnny repeated. "You said, 'Say Johnny,' so I did."

"What a sharp wit," David said, laughing.

"Yup, Tater Creek, your humor is amazing," Ryker said. "That's what I always liked about you. If you ever get tired of prospectin' you can be an entertainer. Why, you ought to be on the stage. The next one leaves in ten minutes."

Johnny dropped his pan and did a hand stand. Righting himself, he slapped Ryker on the shoulder. "You ought to be on the stage right along with me Toby," he said as all three men chuckled.

"Any news downstream?" David asked.

"Not much," Johnny said. "Three amateursfrom back east were out last week panning, but I don't think they got much. One was a tall, skinny drink of water, all Adam's apple and kneecaps. When he panned, he looked like a slough pump out there in the creek bobbing up and down. The other one was husky but didn't have no hair. Looked like he'd been scalped. The third was a runt like me. He was eager to get up to Rochford and see some gal he called Betsy, whoever the heck she is. They all seemed more interested in drinking beer and playing cards anyway. Pleasant fellows though. Shared their beer, played Up and Down the River poker with me, and decorated a bush with the empty beer bottles, they did. Kind of pretty. That's about it…Oh, the widow Crawford's dog had pups, but they all up and died and the old bitch, um, I mean the mother dog died too. After that, the widow was sick abed for quite a while. She's better now. I tended to her for a spell."

"That's too bad," Ryker said. "Maybe some kind of plague or something. We done saw some of that in the cavalry, didn't we, David?"

"Yes, that stuff is spread by infected fleas and ticks," David said. "It can be very serious." Both men appreciated that Potato Creek Johnny undoubtedly saved the life of the widow Crawford out of the goodness of his heart simply because that was the kind of person he was.

"Good thing it was contained," Ryker said. He winked at David and fingered the nugget in his pocket. "Well, guess we best be moseying along, Johnny."

David led Potato Creek Johnny away from his pan, allowing Ryker to sneak up to it. "There is a question I have, Johnny." David bent to the stream and picked up a piece of quartz. "Do you find much of this in the creek bed?" As he spoke, Ryker removed the nugget and placed it directly under Johnny's gold pan, imbedded in the creek with just the tip sticking out of the water.

"Quite a bit," Johnny said. "That and pyrite. At first glance the pyrite in the quartz looks just like gold, but when I scratch it with my knife, it isn't soft like gold."

"Keep working the tailings from the old flume," David suggested. "Before we got the stamp mill, we washed a lot of stone down with gold in it. You may be able to recover some. There may even be some smaller nuggets and placer flakes that were missed."

"Thanks, I'll be sure to do that."

Ryker stood back in place and nodded at David. "Well, Johnny, we got to be heading back yonder to the mine," David said. He and Ryker headed for the buckboard.

"See you," Johnny said, returning to his pan. Before David and Ryker were seated in the buckboard, Johnny let out with a whoop. He jumped out of Horse Creek, did a back flip, and laughed hysterically, flashing the nugget at the men. "Lookee what I found!"

"That big? It must be fool's gold," David said, nudging Ryker.

"This isn't any fool's gold, that's for darn sure," Johnny said. "This is the real thing. Whoppee!"

"Let's get a look at that." Ryker eyed the nugget as Johnny handed it over and whistled. "It's a beauty, all right. That's gold, Johnny."

"It was right under my pan! Right where I laid it when you two came up. The water eddying under there must have exposed the tip. I never would have spotted it otherwise."

"Yeah, I reckon that's what happened all right," Ryker said. "What you going to do with it?"

"Going to go into Deadwood and buy me a nice, big, juicy beefsteak then I'm going to the saloon and buy me a bottle and then I'm going to gamble a bit," Johnny said. "This ought to go a hundred dollars or better and I'm going to spend half of it or die trying."

"Sounds like a good idea," David said. "Enjoy yourself, Johnny."

"I will, and come back and visit real soon," Johnny said. "You bring good luck."

"That we will," Ryker said as they rode off in the buckboard.

Many times thereafter, David would repeat the salting procedure with placer flakes and even tiny nuggets, always suggesting to Johnny he may wish to work a certain area of backwater after the gold was placed. He so enjoyed the enthusiasm the tiny man demonstrated at making his small finds that he felt it was well worth the few dollars in gold he gave away.

"This is so much fun," Laura said as she and Ethan Lattimore rode down the Potato Creek Trail. She was astride Stormy, her paint pony, and he was riding Durango, his bay quarter horse.

"Yeah, I could do this all day," Ethan replied. "We should ride more often."

"I know," Laura said. "I think that every time I go out."

Nearing the limits of Old Deadwood City, Ethan said, "I almost forgot to tell you that Pebbles had pups."

"She did? When?"

"About two weeks back," Ethan said. "Do you want to see them?"

"Sure," Laura replied.

"Let's canter to my place," Ethan said. "They are in the barn."

The two riders arrived at the Lattimore place ten minutes later. Both Laura and Ethan were well-trained horsemen and were careful to allow their geldings to cool down by walking them a ways after dismounting. Only then did they allow the animals to take water.

"I'll take Stormy home and be right back," Laura said.

"Okay." It seemed to Ethan that he had barely removed the tack from Durango when Laura returned. "You're quick."

"I want to play with those pups," Laura said.

"Pebbles had them in here," Ethan said, entering an area of the barn containing hay and feed. They came upon Jenny Lattimore, Ethan's younger sister, sitting with the dogs.

"Hi, Jenny," Laura said.

"Hi," Jenny said back, scratching her arm. "These darn bugs out here are itchy."

"The skeeters out?" Ethan said.

"I don't know," Jenny said, "but Pebbles acts like she's sick."

Both Laura and Ethan squatted to look at the bitch dog that indeed seemed quite listless. She was not interested in nursing. They noticed a half eaten squirrel carcass nearby.

"Where'd that come from?" Ethan said, also slapping at a bug.

"Pebbles dragged it in here a few days back, I guess."

Laura was petting one of the four pups. "They are just darling. I wish I had a dog."

"Take one home," Ethan said. "We'll just give them away anyway or else we'll have to kill them."

"Kill them!" Laura said, holding the puppy protectively.

"Well yeah," Ethan said. "They're mutts, they aren't good for anything. If we can't give them away, we have to kill them. Drown them in a gunny sack most likely."

"Ethan Lattimore, how can you even think such a thing much less say it?" Laura said. She held the pup out toward Ethan. "How can you look into this sweet little face and say such a thing?"

Ethan gulped. "I'm not saying I like it Laura, but if we kept every pup Pebbles pumped out, we'd have fifty dogs running around our yard right now."

"Even so, I —"

"Ethan! Jenny! Suppertime! Oh, hello Laura," Irene Lattimore said upon entering the barn. "Would you like to take that cute little puppy home with you? Maybe his brothers and sisters too so he won't get lonesome." She laughed so heartily that all three of her chins bounced.

"He really is nice, Mrs. Lattimore," Laura said.

"Then take him as a gift," Irene replied. "I don't know much about the father. He was one of those traveling drummer sales dogs that was just passing through." You can tell by the size of the paws how big they will get. He might make a good watchdog for your Pa up at the mine."

"Thanks, Missus Lattimore," Laura said, petting the puppy and smiling. "I'd best get home for supper too or my Pa will give me a good whupping."

"I know your Pa better than that," the chubby Irene Lattimore said. "He's too much of a gentleman to whup you kids."

"Yes, I know," Laura said. "I was just teasing. What should I feed this little guy?"

"He will drink cow's milk watered down a mite," Irene said. "And he's of an age to start eating food too. Maybe soak some bread in water and a little bit of meat chopped up fine."

"Okay, I'll try that," Laura said. "I'll see you tomorrow and let you know how everything is going." She scratched her arm. "Darn gnats."

Running the three doors down to the Stewart mansion, Laura bolted through the back door with the puppy in her arms. "Look at what Ethan gave me Mama," she said breathlessly. "Missus Lattimore said it was all right."

"What a darling little puppy," Ida Mae said, taking the black and white pup into her hands, holding it up, and looking into its face. "They are so cute at this age." She kissed it and nuzzled its face. "I had a pup when I was about your age. We called her Mandy. She was a coal black Heinz Fifty-Seven mutt."

"A puppy!" Pauly said, running up. "Can I hold him! Huh, mom? Can I? Huh? Please?" He pulled on the dog's leg, making it yelp.

"Not right now," Ida Mae scolded. "Here Laura, put him in a box by the stove. You can put an old quilt in there so it will be soft. Then both of you wash up for supper and set the table." She slapped her hands together. "After handling that dog, I'd better wash up too."

After cleaning her hands, Ida Mae proceeded to finish preparing the spaghetti and meat sauce for supper while Laura and Pauly took their turns at the sink then proceeded to set the table. About that time Ryker, who had just returned from his walk, entered the house.

"What have we here?" Ryker said, glancing at the box by the stove. "Looks pretty fearsome to me. Maybe a wild coyote, or a timber wolf even. Be careful of those fangs."

"Just my puppy Grandpa," Laura laughed. "Isn't he cute?"

"He's my puppy too," Pauly grumped.

"He belongs to all of us," Laura said, running her hand lovingly over Pauly's hair then snapping his ear. She was so overcome with excitement at having her very own pup that she had to take her exuberance out on someone. Besides, she hadn't tormented Pauly in a day and a half.

"He's black and white," Pauly said.

"Anyone can see that," Laura said, tweaking Pauly's nose. He pushed her hand away.

"Let's call him Quilt," Pauly said.

Laura shook her head. "That's a dumb name for a dog," she said, stepping on Pauly's foot

"Ouch, quit that, you dimwit!" Pauly shouted, slugging Laura.

"Mama, Pauly called me a dimwit and he hit me," Laura wailed.

"I heard that," Ida Mae said, turning from the stove. "Apologize, Pauly."

"But mom –"

"No buts."

"I'm sorry, Laura."

"That's better," Ida Mae said.

Ryker, who had observed the entire exchange, chuckled to himself. Pauly lost this round but he'd probably win the next one in his ongoing battle with his sister.

"Since I got the dog, I'll name him. I think I'll call him Patches," Laura said as David, fresh from the mine, entered from the barn and saw the pup.

"It came from the Lattimores," Ida Mae said.

David picked up the dog. "Look at the size of those paws. He is going to be big."

"Well, right now our supper is getting cold," Ida Mae said, putting the bowel of spaghetti and the bowl of meat sauce on the table. "Everybody washed up? David, put that dog down and lead us in prayer. Let's eat."

"Oh Lord, we thank you for this food of which we are about to partake, and for our good health and good fortune and for the brotherhood that we share, amen." David said, reaching for the spaghetti.

"Amen," Ida Mae and the others said, heads bowed.

After supper was finished and the dishes cleared, the family adjourned to the parlor where they again turned their attention to the newest addition to the family. Laura gave Patches some warm watered down milk out of an eyedropper that the animal drank readily. It also ate some bread soaked in water and a small amount of spaghetti sauce, but seemed to have a hard time chewing and swallowing the solid food even though it was finely chopped. It voided a bit, which Laura cleaned up. Pauly gave it some more warm milk, which is what it seemed to prefer.

Ryker watched his grandchildren and their pup from the comfort of his rocking chair while David smoked his pipe, read the paper, and chatted with Ida Mae about the day at the mine. He noticed the pup seemed a bit listless and had some matter in its eyes. As far as the listlessness, that could be that it was just tired from being played with, but the runny eyes…Ryker didn't quite know what to make of that. He was careful not to handle the pup and to wash up thoroughly with strong soap after touching others who had touched it. After he prepared for bed, he looked at the puppy again. It whimpered softly as it slept and its eyes were still oozing. It made Ryker uneasy as he headed upstairs to his bedroom.

CHAPTER FOURTEEN

The next morning being Saturday, Laura, accompanied by Grandpa Ryker, hastened to the Lattimores with Patches. They were both dismayed to learn that Pebbles had taken very ill in the night and died, leaving the remaining three puppies with no mother to tend them. Laura readily agreed, even before she secured permission, to take another puppy that she would give to Matthew and Becky. She was just sure they would want a dog, especially with a new baby on the way. The one she took was small and pure white with cocked ears and a moustache.

"I don't know what happened to poor Pebbles," Irene Lattimore said, rubbing her neck. "Oh, I am so gosh awful stiff today. Hope I'm not coming down with something."

"You're just upset over that dog," Gene said. "You were up trying to tend to the mutt half the night." He looked from Ethan and Jenny to Laura and Ryker. "Pebbles was an old dog. She must have been, what, eight, nine...dogs don't live forever, you know. Her time just ran out." He motioned toward the back yard. "Ethan, we need to bury the carcass today in the garden."

"Okay Pa." Ethan scratched his arm, which had a huge welt on it.

"What is that?" Gene said, inspecting his son's arm.

"I don't know," Ethan said. "Bug bite, I guess. It itches like mad."

"Put some cornhuskers lotion on it," Gene said, 'then come on out to the barn. "Let's get that dog buried."

"I'll help you with it Gene," Ryker said. "Maybe the boy ought to stay inside."

"Okay Toby," Gene said. "The sooner I have her buried the better."

Both men went to the barn and hefted the bitch dog that was now stiff into a wheelbarrow and carted it to the garden. Ryker took note of the half eaten squirrel carcass lying nearby and the fleas that were buzzing around the carrion. "Wait a second Gene," Ryker said, scooping the squirrel remains up with a shovel and throwing it onto the wheelbarrow. "Let's bury this too."

The job completed, the men returned to the house. "Let's go home, Grandpa," Laura said. "I'll give this other pup to Matthew and Becky."

"Matthew from the mine," Mister Lattimore said. "I hope they enjoy it. I know when we get rid of these, the next dog we have will be a male. Then we won't have this problem of disposing of pups every year."

Laura hastened on home and explained to Ida Mae what had happened, leaving Patches with her and taking the smaller pup to Matthew and Becky's house. When she arrived, her brother and sister-in-law were just finishing a leisurely breakfast as they had slept in this Saturday morning. They welcomed the puppy with open arms as Becky often got lonely during the day with Matthew away at the mine. They made a bed for it in the barn though as Becky didn't believe in having a housedog. She decided to name it Mister Hickok, for the mustache reminded her of what pictures of Wild Bill had looked like. Indeed, the pup carried itself fancy like the pistoleer and had that certain flair reminiscent of Deadwood's most famous late citizen who now rested on Mount Moriah.

The rest of the weekend was uneventful at both the Lattimore and the Stewart households. By Tuesday however, both families came down with what appeared to be influenza of some kind except that an itchy rash accompanied it. It struck Ida Mae, Laura and Pauly Stewart, and Ethan and Jenny Lattimore in addition to Irene. Only the men were spared. By Thursday the pups started dying including Patches, but by that time Ida Mae and the children were almost too ill to notice. David questioned whether he should go to the mine that day.

"Everybody is so sick Toby," David said, worried.

"Yeah, we'd best get Doc Taggert up here pronto," Ryker said. "Doctor Flora too."

As they spoke, Matthew entered. "Pa, Toby, Becky is ailing. She's in bed with a fever. Her being due to have the baby so soon and all, I don't like this."

"I'm on my way to get the doctor," David said. "I'll send him over to your place when he's done here."

"Okay," Matthew said. "I'm going back home to tend to Becky as best I know how."

"Keep fluids in her, David said. "Water, broth, and the like. You don't want her to dehydrate."

"Okay Pa."

A short time later, David returned with Doc Taggert. He said Doctor Flora had already gone over to the Lattimore house and would join them as soon as she was finished there.

"Just rest easy, Laura," Doc Taggert said, taking her pulse and checking her glands for signs of swelling. He noted what appeared to be bug bites on her arms.

"I'm so sore," Laura said. "I ache all over."

"I know honey," Doc said. "This sure isn't any fun, but I promise that you will get better soon." He gave her some tonic that was mostly alcohol. "This will help you sleep."

After checking on Ida Mae and Pauly, who were in much the same condition as Laura, Doc joined Ryker and David in the family room. He saw the familiar figure of Doctor Stanford walking toward the house. "Here comes Doctor Flora," Taggert said.

Doctor Stanford reported that the Lattimores had much the same symptoms as the Stewarts only worse. "I fear for Irene," she said. "She is really very ill and has a heart condition anyway, being fat like she is. Her breathing is labored. She may die."

The men looked at each other silently for a moment. "Becky Stewart, Matthew's wife, is ill too," Ryker said. "I think it has something to do with the dogs."

"The dogs?" Doc Taggert said. He and Doctor Stanford looked at each other.

"Yes," Ryker said. "First the Lattimore bitch dog had pups. Then Gene told me she got listless and didn't want to nurse. That dog up and

149

died last Saturday. I helped Gene bury it and saw a dead squirrel carcass near where she littered. And there was fleas all over.m And last week when we talked to Tater Creek Johnny out at the mine, he said there were several dog deaths out there too and that the Widow Crawford came down with something and was real sick for several days. Anyway, we buried the bitch and the squirrel remains, but I'd bet my bottom dollar they all had the plague of some sort." He glanced at David. "We seen that before, didn't we, David."

"Yes and it wasn't a pretty sight," David said.

"And the pups from that bitch, they came into the Lattimore place, into this house, and to Matthew's home," Ryker said.

"Good Lord," Doctor Stanford said. "This is exactly how the plague spreads. It goes through the food chain and through handling of infected specimens and through the infected fleas. The pups would catch it through the bitch's mother's milk."

"There are welts on the children upstairs," Doc Taggert said, shaking his head.

David approached Doc Taggert. "Doc, you mean Laura, Pauly, even Ida Mae…"

Doc nodded. "I'm placing all three residences under quarantine. Everyone here has been exposed. No one is to come or go until I say so. I will post the doors."

Putting his hands to his face, David shook his head in denial. "Oh, no! It can't be!"

"We have to contain this," Doctor Stanford said. "We do know that isolating it will keep it from spreading."

Regaining his composure, David said, "You'd best tell Seth Bullock about this."

"I fully intend to," Doctor Taggert said.

The next three days were horrible in the quarantined households. Doctor Stanford moved into the Lattimore residence to provide what around-the-clock assistance she could. Doctor Taggert informed Seth Bullock of the quarantine and also wired Doctor Valentine McGillycuddy in Rapid City and requested his assistance. McGillycuddy responded within the day and took up residence with Matthew and Becky Stewart. Doc Taggert remained at the Stewart mansion. Even with David and Ryker to assist him, the three men had their hands full.

150

"Breathe easy, Irene." Doctor Stanford listened to Irene Lattimore's chest through her stethoscope. Irene was delirious with fever.

"Irene darling." Gene sat on the bed holding his wife's hand. "Don't leave me. Oh please don't leave me. Hang on." He started to cry.

"Katie, help me," Irene said, opening her eyes and staring at the ceiling. "Angels."

"Katie was her mother," Gene said. He pressed his hands to his face and began to cry.

"She is delusional," Doctor Stanford said. "Her pulse is racing. I'm afraid she is going into heart failure." Five minutes later, Irene Louise Lattimore, age 43, was dead.

"Stewart! David Stewart you son-of-a-bitch, come on out here or we'll burn the mansion down around you!"

Opening the front door just a crack, David stuck his rifle barrel out onto the porch and peered at the mob that had gathered. "I can't come out and you men know it. This house is under quarantine. Now go home. Scat!"

"You brought the plague to Deadwood, you stupid bastard!" a voice shouted.

"You are in no danger," David said. "This is contained."

"Never did like you high and mighty Stewarts," someone hollered.

"Yeah," someone else said, "always actin' hoity-toity like you're better than the rest of us."

"Burn the house down!" another cried.

"It's built of stone. That's pretty hard to do, men." The voice, mild but commanding, was followed by a stick of dynamite which was pitched onto the porch. "You will need this." When everyone looked toward the voice, they saw Toby Ryker step from the side of the house holding a dynamite fuse in one hand and a pistol in the other. He waved the fuse. "But you'll have to go through me to get it." He cocked the pistol. "Now, which one of you hotheaded jackasses is first?"

A silence fell over the crowd of 10 or so, most of who were drunk and talked into this mob action by George "Weenie" Weinstein, a horse trader and sometime gambler at the Number 10 Saloon. While the men contemplated their next move, the sound of a Winchester levering a cartridge drew their attention. "Seth Bullock on this side boys. You want to go ahead and make your play, have at it. I've got plenty of shells and you are like ducks sitting on the water out here."

"Hey Weenie, what do we do now?" Angus Cuthbert, one of the mob said.

"Aye, Weinstein, ye suck hen's eggs!" Colin McShane yelled in his thick brogue. "I'm freezin' me hinder off out here!"

"Yeah, what the heck you talk us into this for anyway?" Marlow Pruitt, another drunk replied. "It's cold out here and my beer's getting warm back in the Number Ten."

"You men, if you can call yourselves that, ought to be downright ashamed of yourselves," Ryker said. "David Stewart and his family are the best thing that ever happened to this dump of a town. They pay taxes, they support this town, they work the Potato Creek Mine, and Ida Mae, who lies sick nearly to death in the bedroom upstairs at this very minute, teaches your children the necessaries of life out of the goodness of her heart. And I can tell you this, if this predicament was reversed and it was you who was sick, Ida Mae would be there to tend to you and to offer you her help. She wouldn't be standing in front of your house threatening to burn you out. I know what I'm talking about because she saved my life many times over." Ryker scoffed. "You're right about one thing though. The Stewarts are better than you trash deserve." He fired into the air. "Now get going!"

"It seemed like a right good idea at the saloon," Weenie said. "We're sorry."

"That you look," Ryker replied.

"Is there anything we can do to help out?" Angus Cuthbert said.

"Yes, get some warm food over here," Ryker said. "And some over to the Lattimores, and over to my grandson Matthew Stewart's house too. And lots of fresh water and milk and maybe some brandy."

"It shall be done," Angus Cuthbert said. "My woman makes the best chicken noodle soup you ever tasted. It's comforting when you're sick."

"Mine does up a mean German potato salad," another said.

Colin McShane swallowed the last of his bottle. "Some hearty mate finished this one off, otherwise ye could have it," he said, tossing the empty brandy bottle aside. "But there's another brandy jug to home. Be bringing it over to ye directly."

"We got the fixings for pot roast," Marlow Pruitt said as the crowd began to disburse.

"Ryker, you sure know how to work a crowd," Seth said. He shook Ryker's hand while he watched the crowd walk away. "I'm amazed, plumb amazed."

"They anger me," Ryker said, holstering his gun. "Honestly, talking that way about my family!" He looked at Seth, his jaws clenching. "In the olden days, I would have pounded the crap out of them just to teach them a lesson."

"I think you got the message across," Seth said, patting Ryker on the shoulder. "Now you best get back inside. You are part of the quarantine too, you know."

"Yes sir," Ryker said, heading toward the door.

"David," Seth said, tipping his hat. "I'll keep an eye on the place, but I don't think you'll have any more trouble after what Ryker did."

"I agree," David replied. "He is amazing. Well, I got to get back inside too, Seth. Time to check on the family again. Oh by the way, could you bring over three or four chamber pots from the store? They'd come in mighty handy."

"Sure, I'll drop them off on my way home tonight."

Within 3 hours there was a turnout of well-wishers at the homes of the stricken that was unsurpassed at any time in Deadwood. They were saddened to hear of the passing of Irene Lattimore and helped a grief-stricken Gene make the funeral arrangements with Magellan Fry. The churches got involved by cooking meals for the families in their kitchens. What the Stewarts and the Lattimores couldn't use, the churches served to the public, requesting a free-will offering with the proceeds to go to charity. By the second day of the siege, Ida Mae, Laura, and Pauly were all purging, vomiting and dehydrated, alternating between fevers and chills and sick nearly to death. Ryker and David assisted Doc Taggert in tending to them by putting cool washcloths on their foreheads when feverish and warming their feet when chilled and giving them sponge baths between meals. And fluids, they pushed fluids night and day even though it seemed to pass right through the victims of the plague. But as the doctor explained, they needed to keep from dehydrating and they needed to keep their strength up.

"Whew!" Ryker said, entering the front room after emptying the chamber pots. "I'm getting too old for this."

"We all are," David said. "Right now though, they are all resting comfortably for the first time since this all started."

Doc Taggert joined the men in the front room. "I think the worst is over. They are very weak, but I think they all three burned the plague out of their systems."

"Doc," Ryker said, "you mean…"

"Yes, they will all pull through. Give them lots of buttermilk and yogurt. It will help to improve the function of their gut."

"Praise the Lord," David said, shedding a tear. "If that's what it takes, we'll pump yogurt down them until it's coming out of their ears."

Ryker, crying also, hugged David and the doctor. "This is the best news I ever heard in my whole darn life. Thanks, Doc. I owe you one."

"We are very fortunate," Doc said. "But there is still the Lattimore children and Becky Stewart. I'm going to check with Doctor Stanford and Doctor McGillycuddy and see how they are doing. I'll be back in a couple of hours."

Doc Taggert's prediction came to pass. The following day, Ida Mae, Laura and Pauly all had their fevers break. They were still weak and had lost much weight but they developed ravenous appetites, which Doc said was a good sign. They were on the mend.

"Ida Mae, I was so worried," David said, kissing her hand.

"There isn't a lot of it I even remember," Ida Mae said weakly. She sat in the rocker in the master bedroom now, a tray of food before her, which she partook of heartily. "This is good sour kraut," she said. "Who made it?"

"The church folks delivered it," David said. "They have been wonderful through all this, Ida Mae. It is heart-warming to see how much they love you and the children."

Ida Mae passed gas. "Oops," she said demurely.

"Well, that end is working fine," David said, chuckling.

"Like my father always said, you can't keep anything you can't hold in your hand," Ida Mae replied.

"You got your humor back," David said. "That's wonderful."

"I'm so sore that it feels as though someone ran a scrub brush through my innards. If I never see another chamber pot for the rest of my life, it will suit me just fine."

"Laura, Pauly, how are you feeling?" Ryker said in the next room.

"Lousy," Laura said, letting her tongue hang out.

"Like I been gut shot," Pauly said.

"Oh?" Ryker replied. "And how many times have you been gut shot, Pauly?"

"Right now, it feels like ten."

"Well, you don't know how tickled your Ma and Pa and I are that you're takin' nourishment. How about some of this chicken tremendous, the church ladies call it?" Ryker smelled the casserole. "Smells delicious. Chicken and mushroom soup over a bed of rice."

"Gimme some," Pauly said. "I want a drumstick. Betcha Chen would like this."

"One drumstick coming up."

"I will have some breast meat please," Laura said.

After Ryker served the two children, he sat back and enjoyed watching them eat.

"This is good," Pauly said, his cheeks bulging.

"There's no hurry, so you can just take your time," Ryker said.

"Grandpa, where's Patches?" Laura asked.

Ryker moved in and hugged the girl. "Honey, I'm afraid Patches isn't with us anymore. It was those puppies of the Lattimores that carried the disease that made you so sick. Those puppies all died just like Pebbles."

Laura pounded her head and began to cry. "I could have killed the whole family just because of a stupid dog."

"Shush now," Ryker said, cuddling her and patting her back. "You had no way of knowing that. It wasn't your fault."

"I heard them say Missus Lattimore died," Laura sobbed.

"Yes she did, honey."

"How about Ethan and Jenny and Matthew and Becky and…" her eyes grew wide, "the baby!"

"Don't know about them just yet," Ryker said. "Doc Taggert is checking on them now."

A few hours later, Doc Taggert returned to the Stewart mansion and joined David and Ryker in Ida Mae's bedroom. "Matthew's Becky is recovering well. She had a bad cold and a touch of the flu and not what you and the Lattimores suffered, although their pup had it and died. Luckily they didn't allow it into the house." He smiled. "While I was there, she was delivering a healthy baby girl."

"That's wonderful," Ida Mae said.

"Our first grandchild," David said, hugging her.

"This makes me a great grandpa," Ryker said.

"Ethan Lattimore is coming out of it fine," Doc said. "He is a strong boy. His little sister Jenny isn't doing very well though. I doubt she will last the night."

"This is so sad," Ryker said. "A young one like her ought to have a chance at life. Us old duffers have had our day, but one her age…I'd trade places with her if I could."

"It would take a miracle," Doc said. "When she heard her mama died she just gave up. That's the worst of it. She isn't even trying to fight off this illness."

"Doc, is there a chance if she got her dander up?" Ryker asked.

"I'd say so," Doc said. "Slim but yes, I'd say so."

"Can I go over there and help tend to her?"

"I guess it would be all right. Tell Doctor Stanford I authorized it."

"Thanks, Doc." With that, Ryker went to his trunk, took something out of it, threw on a coat and headed out into the night.

"Gene?" Ryker shook Gene Lattimore awake. "Gene, why don't you go to bed and get a decent night's sleep. Doctor Flora and I will tend to Jenny tonight."

"What? Oh, hello Toby. Okay, thank you. How's your family?"

"They are coming along just fine."

"Good, that's good. Magellan is holding Irene over for burial til the day after tomorrow." Gene's eyes grew misty. "Maybe there will be a double funeral."

"Don't think that way Gene," Ryker said. "You rest now."

"Okay, call me if there is any change with my Jennifer."

"I will."

Ryker entered the sick room where Doctor Flora sat next to Jenny Lattimore. The small frail girl, pale as alabaster, looked like a china doll lying in the bed. He fought off his inclination to cuddle her, to soothe her, for he knew sympathy was not what she needed. Jenny was supplying herself with a near-fatal dose of that already. He prepared himself to shock her out of her lethargy with harshness, figuring that was the only chance she had to come through this siege alive.

"She won't eat," Doctor Flora said.

"Is she awake?" Ryker asked.

"Yes but unresponsive. The fever has broken and technically she has beaten the disease, but she's lost the will to live since her mother died. I can treat her body but I don't know how to treat her mind."

"Good," Ryker said. "Can I be alone with her? And leave some food and broth here."

"I'll be outside," Doctor Flora said.

Once they were alone, Ryker fell to work. The first thing he did was put on a long somber face and hum *The Streets of Larado* to himself while measuring Jenny from various angles with a tape. At first she ignored him and he ignored her. Finally, her curiosity got the better of her and she began to watch him. He jotted down a few notes then began to rummage through her closet. He pulled out dresses and toys, looked at them, muttered, "junk" or "how ugly" and tossed them aside. Grabbing Jenny's doll off the bed, he looked it all over then opened the window and tossed it out.

"Hey! What are you doing?" Jenny said at last.

Ryker looked at Jenny as though seeing her for the first time. He dropped his voice to a low dull monotone. "Ain't you dead yet? Hurry up and die then, Jenny Lattimore. I'm here to measure you for your coffin and I don't have all night. Meanwhile I'll pick out the dress to bury you in. And that doll, nobody will be needing that ugly thing anymore."

"That's my dolly," Jenny said. "And you look like Grandpa Toby Ryker Stewart to me."

"Grandpa Toby Ryker Stewart? Who is that? My name's Percival Welander from Saint Paul, and where you're going there aren't any stupid ugly dolls allowed."

Jenny stuck out her lip. "My Mama's dead and you are a mean old man. Can't you just let me alone so I can die too?"

"Shut up and die then, you selfish snot-nosed brat."

"Selfish? What do you mean?" Jenny's lips were beginning to tremble with emotion and she was beginning to get tears in her eyes.

"I mean there you lie, a beautiful little girl with the whole world at your feet, a father who loves you more than his own life itself, a big brother who needs you, and all you can think of is dying. Yes, you are a selfish brat. What do you think will happen to them when you give up and let yourself die?"

"They let Mama die."

"They did not. Your mama was a wonderful woman who died because she was not able to fight back." Ryker shook his finger at Jenny. "You don't have that excuse. You can fight back. You just don't care enough to, and that is a disgrace to your mama's memory." He picked up a family picture off the dresser taken months before. "She's looking down at you from heaven right now just like she's looking at you from this picture, and shamed she is to be the mother of such a selfish girl. And speaking of shame, it is you who should be ashamed of yourself, Jenny Lattimore. But why should I care? Hurry up and die, you selfish brat."

Jenny sat up in bed and crossed her arms, staring at Ryker as he picked up another dress. "This will look fine," he said. "You will look okay after we pump you full of juice and put wax all over your face and glue your eyes shut forever. Course, the worms will crawl into your coffin in a day or two anyway. Now I'll find an outfit to bury your brother and your father in too. When they see you giving up hope, they will too. You Lattimores are weaklings. The world is better off rid of you. I'll stick the whole bunch of you in the ground."

"No!" Jenny screamed then she broke down and began to sob. "Daddy and Ethan won't die. We Lattimores are strong." She shuddered. "And I hate worms! Get away from me, you ugly old monster!" She kicked at him with what little strength she had.

"Ha! You think you can fight me, Jenny Lattimore," Ryker said, holding out a cup of broth. "Nobody can fight me, but if you want to try it, you can start with this. I dare you to." He crossed his arms and laughed at her as she drank, picked up the tape, and left the room, instantly replaced by Doctor Stanford.

An hour later, Jenny Lattimore was a changed child. Her will to live was restored and she had a mission in life, a mission to make a home for her father and brother now that her mama was no longer able to do so. She ate a decent meal, kept it all down, and although it would take her several days to fully recover, Jenny would do just that. Percival Welander mysteriously disappeared after that one meeting and when Ryker re-entered Jenny's bedroom to relieve Doctor Stanford, the girl told him about the cruel man.

"He said what?" Ryker roared. "Where is he? I'll get my gun."

"He's gone now," Jenny said, half smiling at Ryker's flamboyant reaction. "But he looked just like you, only he talked odd and creepy."

"Maybe he was a dream," Ryker said.

"Maybe," Jenny said "He could have been a dream, I don't know, but he measured me for a coffin."

Ryker stared at Jenny. His jaw dropped and his eyes widened. "Percival Welander," he whispered.

"That is what he said his name was," Jenny replied, her eyes widening too.

"The phantom undertaker from Saint Paul was here?"

"Yes, and he looked just like you but he talked funny."

"I've heard of him," Ryker said. "He's a powerful old ghost who's doomed to roam the west in search of bodies on whom to practice his embalming art. Word has it only one other person ever escaped death once he appeared to them and that was Paul Bunyon, the giant lumberjack. How did you ever manage to get away from him?"

"I told him daddy and Ethan and I were strong and I told him to get away from me, that's how," Jenny said. "Then he gave me some broth and dared me to drink it and left. I scared that ugly old ghost away."

"Well now I just bet you did darling," Ryker said, punching her playfully on the arm. "You are one tough girl."

"Yup, but I'm glad he's gone and you are here." She hugged Ryker then rubbed her stomach. "I'm hungry again."

"Wonderful," Ryker said. "I'll get you some soup and crackers and some pot roast made by Marlow Pruitt, a dear friend of mine from the Number Ten Saloon."

"Mister Ryker, this is amazing," Doctor Flora said after closing the door of Jenny's room. The child was now sleeping peacefully. "I think she will be all right now. How did you do it?"

"Let's just say I know a bit about how girls that age think," Ryker said.

"With your weakened condition, it's fortunate you did not contract this," Doctor Flora said.

"Was mighty careful around it," Ryker replied. "Learned to respect the plague while I served in the cavalry."

He spent much time with Jenny over the next few weeks, encouraging her every step of the way and providing inspiration when needed. Out of that closeness grew a bond between Ryker and Jenny Lattimore that was just as intense as one had been between a mountain man and a small girl in a Pawnee tipi many years before.

CHAPTER FIFTEEN

The families of David Stewart, Eugene Lattimore, and Matthew Stewart wish to extend our heartfelt appreciation for the kindness bestowed upon us by the by the ladies and gentlemen of the Deadwood community during our recent siege with illness and with your support at the death of our sister, Irene Lattimore. In appreciation, a potluck roast beef barbecue will be served at the David Stewart residence this coming Saturday June 15th come rain or come shine, commencing at 12:00 noon. Please bring a dish to pass, but no pets allowed.

The invitation appeared in the classified advertising section of the Deadwood paper three weeks after the siege began which claimed the life of Irene Lattimore and nearly that of her daughter. When the day arrived, Juan Carlos Lopez, whom Ryker had learned of from Esmeralda Krump and told Ida Mae about, arrived with a full beef cooked on a spit. Ida Mae had contracted with the Mexican to cater the affair.

"Told ya Juan Lopez came recommended highly," Ryker said, helping David and Matthew move a picnic table into place on the lawn.

"That beef smells delicious," David said.

"It's Hereford, not longhorn," Ryker said, chuckling at the memory of Big Nose Charlie.

"Becky and I have eaten at his restaurant," Matthew said. "Becky likes his tortillas."

"I recollect Esmeralda saying he made a good tortilla," Ryker said.

"Esmeralda?" David said, winking at Matthew.

"Just never you mind," Ryker said. "Just never you mind. Oh, there she is." Esmeralda and Camille had joined Juan and his children for the festivities and to help serve the beef.

"*Ola, Senor Ryker*," she said as Ryker waved back.

"Esmeralda, good to see you again," Ryker said, looking down his nose at David and Matthew.

The afternoon was pleasant with nearly 200 guests making an appearance. Seth Bullock, Doctors Taggert and Stanford, Potato Creek Johnny, Hiram and Prudence Custis, Poker Alice and even Calamity Jane stopped by, and Seth Bullock managed to get in a short speech. David got a couple kegs of beer for those who wished to imbibe and set them up in one corner of the yard. About mid-afternoon, Axel and Lucille Brown and the boys showed up, oohing and aahing over Becky and their firstborn granddaughter.

"Oh, isn't little Lucille a sweetheart," Lucille Brown said.

"Yes Ma, but that won't be her name," Becky said.

Lucille continued to fuss with the baby, ignoring her daughter. "Hello Ida Mae," she said as Missus Stewart approached. "My goodness gracious, such an ordeal you went through! Sick nearly to death, I hear. Were you in great pain?"

"It was gruesome," Ida Mae said, knowing Lucille enjoyed hanging on every miserable word. "I still get twinges. In fact, I had a large one just now as you came up. During the ordeal, I suffered the anguish of the lepers of old."

"Oh dear," Lucille said. "Did you repent your sinful ways?"

"Many times, Lucille. I swore that if I lived through this, I would do penance for the rest of my life."

"I notice David is serving beer," Lucille said.

"He has not yet seen the light, Lucille," Ida Mae said. "Please pray for him."

"Oh, I shall," Lucille said, heading toward Juan with a plate. "Hey, burrito boy, what you got cookin'?"

"What a darling baby," Ida Mae said, also admiring her granddaughter.

"Axel, you old rattlesnake, where have you been keeping yourself?" David said as Axel Brown approached the plank sitting atop the two kegs that made a makeshift bar.

"Out to home blacksmithing," Axel said, quaffing a beer. "I've been making some trivets for Bullock and Star Hardware that they sell to the ladies in town." He leaned toward David. "Made the jigs myself. I can make up a trivet in about twenty minutes or so. The bird designs are the most popular. Cost me about four cents to make. I sell them to Bullock for eight cents and he sells them thirteen cents apiece or two for a quarter. We can't keep them in stock."

"You're making a tidy profit," David said.

"It's all in how you merchandise the product, and if you are the only producer, you can name your price."

Matthew joined the conversation as Axel chatted. "Do you know how to make a horse shoe, Papa Brown?"

"What's that?"

"Well, it's "U" shaped and fits on a horse's hoof. Most blacksmiths know how to make them."

"Never heard of the blasted things," Axel said, chuckling.

"Where are the boys?" David said.

"They are coming along," Axel said. "They plan to sing a few tunes if it's all right with you. If anyone wants to pitch a penny or two into the guitar case, that would please them."

"Sure, they can have at it," David said as Ryker approached.

"Axel," Ryker said.

"That's my name. Don't wear it out or your wheels will fall off."

Ryker laughed, slapping his knee. "You got a mind like greased lightening, Axel."

"Oh, axle grease huh?" Axel said.

"Stop," Ryker hooted. "You'll give me the apoplexy." He was still chuckling as Ida Mae, Gene Lattimore, and Jenny approached.

"Axel," Ida Mae said.

"That's my name. Don't wear it out or your wheels will fall off." Ryker had to sit down, he was laughing so hard.

"I'm surprised to see you drinking a beer," Ida Mae said. "What will Lucille think of this?"

"Oh, we have an understanding," Axel said.

"An understanding?"

"Yes, she understands that she can't drink anything and has to suffer for both her transgressions and mine and I understand I have to drink and carry on so she has something to suffer about." He downed half the mug of beer. "It works out quite satisfactorily for both of us."

"How's it going for you, Gene?" Ryker said. With one arm he patted Gene Lattimore on the back, and with the other he hugged Jenny Lattimore who looked up at him and hugged him back just as hard as she could. "Good to see you up and about, darling."

"Thanks Grandpa Ryker Stewart," Jenny said. "I love you."

"I love you, too, honey," Ryker said, bending down and kissing her.

"Jenny's coming along fine," Gene said. "I'm getting used to being without Irene but it still hurts." He looked away and bit his lip. "But folks have been wonderful. They're still coming over and bringing food and helping out."

"Things like this can not only bring out the worst in folks, like that mob at our place, but the best in them too," Ryker said.

The Brown boys set up along the other side of the yard and struck up a lively version of *Yankee Doodle* followed by the mellow ballad *Shenandoah,* and were pleased to see several people drop not pennies but nickels into their guitar case. Then they sang *Bringing in the Sheaves* to appease their mother, but were dismayed to see everyone walk away so they decided not to do any more hymns today. They switched back to the *Old Folks at Home, Dixie*, and *Oh Susannah* and were making coin again.

Laura Stewart and Ethan Lattimore stood side by side and sang along with the boys while clapping their hands to *Oh, Susannah*. When the boys took a break, they approached Jeremiah.

"That was fun," Laura said.

"We've been working hard at it and writing our own songs too," Jeremiah said.

"Well, your day will come," Laura said.

"Our day wi-ill come," Jeremiah sang, strumming his guitar. He looked at Laura in anticipation.

"Nope," Laura said.

"Yeah, guess you're right," Jeremiah said.

"But your day will come," Laura said. "Don't give up."

"To everything there is a season," Ethan said as he and Laura waved and walked away.

"Hey, that's from the good book." Jeremiah began to strum and sang, "To ev-ery-thing, ya, ya, ya, there is a sea-son, ya, ya, ya." He sighed. "Nope, that won't work either. Geez, this songwriting is hard."

"I was so sick," Pauly said to Chen. The two visited while sitting on the grass sharing a whole apple pie. "I threw up all the time and some-times it was even green."

"That's awful," Chen said, taking another bite. "So, tell me more."

"Well, I remember this other time I started feeling sick and..."

"Ida Mae," Doc Taggert said elsewhere in the yard. "You look radi-ant."

"Thanks Norman, I'm feeling much better. I appreciate your help through all of this. You and Doctor Flora were magnificent."

"Thank you, Ida Mae. It is all in a day's work, and thank you for paying the bill so promptly. That is something we doctors are not used to."

"Ida Mae," Seth Bullock said as he moseyed up to her with a plate full of food. "This is good beef."

"So I've heard," Ida Mae replied. I haven't tried any yet, but Toby Ryker assures us that Juan Lopez is an excellent cook."

"He certainly is that."

"I appreciate all your assistance, Seth. Not only with seeing us through the plague, but with the Cobb gang as well."

"Think nothing of it," Bullock replied. "It goes with the badge, and both David and Matthew were a big help to me."

"What made the Cobbs do it, Seth?"

"Well, I tell ya – "

"Hi Seth!" Calamity Jane interrupted. She pulled out her .45, twirled it around her finger, and fired into the air.

"Jane, holster the gun." Seth rested his hand on his six-shooter. "How much have you had to drink this morning?"

"Just a little nip to ward off the plague, Seth. Honest."

"You know better than to be firing a gun here in this crowd. You're liable to hit someone. Then I'd have to shoot you right between the eyes, not that it would hurt you any."

Undaunted by Seth's harsh words, Jane put her gun away and smiled at the marshal. "How the hell you been, you big old shithead?"

"Just fine Jane, you delicate little flower, you. I was just explaining to Ida Mae about the Cobbs and their ilk…" Seth launched into a political speech that caught the ears of several passersby. George "Weenie" Weinstein, Marlow Pruitt, Colin McShane and the other boys from the bar, beers in hand, crowded around him and nodded supportively as he spoke.

Poker Alice Tubbs approached Ida Mae quietly. "Good day to you, Missus Stewart, ah, Ida Mae," she whispered, not wanting to call attention to herself nor interfere with Seth's speech. The marshal was really cranking himself up as he expounded on the Cobbs and the other significant gossip of the day. And he had an opinion on how to fix everything that needed tending to in Deadwood regardless of what it was.

Ida Mae grew weary of Seth's speech and since he was entertaining a receptive audience, she backed away. "Hello Alice. I'm so happy you could attend our shinding."

"Took some time off from the Number Ten," Alice replied as she lit up a cigar. "I wouldn't miss this for the world. Say, by the way, where is that new grandchild of yours?"

"Right over there." Ida Mae pointed through the crowd at Matthew and Becky. "Come on, I'll introduce you." The two women headed in that direction and were joined by Ryker and David en route. "This is our first grandchild," Ida Mae said. "Matthew, Becky, I believe you know Missus Tubbs." As she said it, Ryker and David shook hands with the cigar-smoking poker player and said their hellos.

"Sure do. Hi Alice," Matthew said.

"Howdy Matthew," Alice replied. "That's one beautiful baby you and Becky have there."

"Fortunately she favors her mother," Matthew joked.

"I see some Stewart in him too," Ida Mae said. "What do you think, Grandpa David?"

David picked up the chubby pink baby, careful to support her neck. "No, I think she looks like that fellow who lives next door to you folks Matthew," he said, chuckling. "You know, the one who came out from Faribault Minnesota and plans to start a transportation system for the school kids of Deadwood."

"Oh that guy," Matthew said. "Yeah, kind of like a dray line for people. He's a dreamer. Who would ever pay to have their kids hauled to school?"

"Good question," David said. "Why, when I was a kid I had to walk five miles to school and five miles back home again and it was uphill both ways.

"Well, there is no doubt about who the father is," Becky said, interrupting David and Matthew before the baloney got any thicker. "Just watch her eat sometime. She has Matthew's appetite."

David passed the baby to Ryker, who took her carefully and cradled her in his arms. "My great granddaughter," was all he said. He cooed at the infant as she clasped his finger with a tiny hand then kissed her forehead, not noticing the family smiling at him. "You kids done good," he said, handing the baby back to Becky. "What are you going to call her?"

"Our baby is going to be named Ida Mae in remembrance of the most wonderful woman in my life," Becky said.

"I'm indeed honored," Ida Mae said.

Ryker nodded approvingly at the family and sighed. In all his years he never seemed as contented as he did right now. Everything seemed just right. He exchanged handshakes and hugs all around, and as the festivities were beginning to break up anyway, he excused himself and went out for his walk. By the time he returned, Matthew and Becky and baby Ida Mae were about to go home and the rest of the family was settling in for the evening. He stood in the yard and looked around then stretched and touched his toes. A subtle weariness overcame him as the warm sun beat down from the blue sky, now dotted with billowy white clouds. Moving over to the hammock that David had stretched between two trees the previous week, he stretched out upon it and gazed at two bald eagles as they danced in the air. He thought about taking a pill, but dismissed it from his mind. Smiling, his eyes drifted shut and he saw Wild Flower and Hope with a bright light behind them beckoning to him. They seemed so close that he could almost touch them. He remembered reaching out to them and them reaching back just before they all three blended into the light.

"Where's Grandpa Ryker?" Matthew said a few minutes later. "I want to say goodbye to him before we leave."

"Think I saw him return from his walk," David replied. "He's probably outside. Let's check." The two men stepped outside and saw the familiar figure lying in the hammock.

"Grandpa Ryker, Becky and I are going home now," Matthew said, touching the old man. There was no response. "Grandpa Ryker?" Matthew shook him harder. "Grandpa Ryker!" He turned to his father. "Pa, I think Grandpa Ryker has gone to a better place."

David moved to Ryker's side and checked his pulse both at his wrist and at his neck and then removed his hat and placed his ear to the old man's chest. "I'm afraid you are right son," he said, standing, glancing into the distance and sighing. "Toby had that lawyer update his will, Matt. Gave me a copy the other day." He smiled at Matthew through his tears. "Told me he went ahead and bought a family plot and to bury him on Mount Moriah."

Matthew too shed a tear as father and son hugged then gazed upon the still form in the hammock. "Grandpa kept saying he wanted everything in order, Pa."

"He got his wish," David said. "And in the process, Toby also taught us how to live right and proper."

Nodding, Matthew added, "And he also taught us how to die right and proper."

High overhead, a shaft of sunlight pushed through the clouds, bringing with it a warm light to the men. With the warmth and light came the scream of an eagle as it lit from its nest and glided upwards on the rising currents of air. David Stewart gazed at Ryker, lying in peaceful repose. His face still carried a smile, which was unusual, for in death, an ordinary man's muscles relaxed, expressionless. But then, David knew that nothing about Toby Ryker had been ordinary. Glancing skyward, the eagle reminded him of the old man's previous words: *Oh, look at the king of the skies, David. Sailing and soaring above his domain. Like a free spirit rising, he is. When it's all over for me, here, I hope that is the feeling I'll have.* David sensed that Ryker's spirit was now one with that eagle, freed from the bonds of earthly concerns, and took comfort in knowing this was the way the mountain man wanted it to end. He sighed, replaced his hat, and squinted at the bird until it disappeared from view.

www.ingramcontent.com/pod-product-compliance
Lightning Source LLC
Chambersburg PA
CBHW052132170626
46812CB00004B/1367